THE SILVER LINING

AMANDA SPOTTISWOODE

ILLUSTRATIONS *by* MOLLY MARCH

Victoria | Vancouver | Calgary

Heritage House Publishing Company Ltd.
heritagehouse.ca

Cataloguing information available from Library and Archives Canada
978-1-77203-132-4 (pbk)
978-1-77203-133-1 (epub)
978-1-77203-134-8 (epdf)

Edited by Lara Kordic
Proofread by Lenore Hietkamp
Cover illustrations by Molly March
Interior book design by Setareh Ashrafologhalai
Back cover design by Jacqui Thomas

The interior of this book was produced on 100%
post-consumer recycled paper, processed chlorine
free and printed with vegetable-based inks.

We acknowledge the financial support of the Government
of Canada through the Canada Book Fund (CBF) and the
Canada Council for the Arts, and the Province of
British Columbia through the British Columbia Arts
Council and the Book Publishing Tax Credit.

20 19 18 17 16 1 2 3 4 5

Printed in Canada

For Jasper

CONTENTS

AUTHOR'S NOTE

Some of the places and people I write about in this book are based on real places and people, though I have altered some details to fit the story. The Quilchena Hotel opened in 1908 and closed its doors to the public in 1920. It remained a private home for the next forty years, before reopening as a hotel in the 1960s. In the story, I have made it an operating hotel in 1938. I stayed at the Quilchena in 1977, when a room cost fourteen dollars, and I remember being fascinated by the bullet holes in the hotel bar! I went riding up in the hills behind the hotel and saw several abandoned silver mines. Because of that experience, I imagined my fictional children and Captain Gunn staying in that grand old building and exploring silver mines on their journey. Regardless of whether it was a hotel or a home, it remains a great historical landmark.

The High Farm is also a real place. Friends of mine have lived there for more than thirty years. The unusual round barn at Fintry still stands in what is now a provincial park, but the orchards and cattle are long gone.

Joe Coultee, Frank and Kenny Ward, the Laird of Fintry, and Tierney O'Keefe are all people who were alive and well and living in the Merritt/Okanagan area in 1938. Jim Richardson and Jim Spilsbury were both pioneer aviators of the era, though I have started Jim Spilsbury's career a few years before he actually began flying. It was my good fortune that so many interesting people were living in the exact time that I wanted to set this story, which takes place two years after the adventure in my first book, *Brother XII's Treasure*. All the other characters, including Captain Gunn and the children, are entirely fictional.

PROLOGUE

April 20, 1938

Dear Molly and Leticia,

How would you feel about another Canadian adventure? Knowing you the way I do, I'm fairly certain that the answer to that question will be a resounding "Yes!"

I have an idea for an adventure, but I'm not going to spoil the fun by laying all my cards on the table. Your mother, Mrs. Phillips, and I have already been in correspondence and have agreed to let you loose once again on the unsuspecting Canadian public. Fortunately, Sophie has proved to be responsible beyond her years, otherwise your respective mothers might not be so keen on allowing these transatlantic adventures. Remember this and give Sophie the respect she deserves.

You will be boarding the *Empress of Britain* a few days after school term finishes in the middle of July, and you'll be back in England for the start of the autumn term at the end of September. Canada still does not have official passenger travel on airplanes, but I think I can convince our old friend Jim Richardson to fly you on one of his freight runs from Montreal to Vancouver since he got some wonderful publicity out of your last flight with him. You are a lucky bunch!

I look forward to seeing you in Vancouver.

All the best from your Uncle Bert
c.c. Mark, Sophie, Harriet, and Posy

April 26, 1938

AN CUILEANN
Plockton
Scotland

Dear Uncle Bert,

We are packing already! Mother is making us bring pretty dresses again for the ocean voyage, but we are sure that whatever adventure you have planned for us won't involve getting dressed up! Too bad you won't tell us what we'll be up to, but we suppose not knowing is part of the fun!

Sophie, Harriet, Mark, and Posy are thrilled, too, and we MacTavishes have agreed to be particularly nice to Sophie and not tease her too much about being responsible and organized! You really are the best uncle ever!

Your loving nieces, Molly and Leticia

CHAPTER ONE

THE START OF ANOTHER ADVENTURE

Summer 1938

The huge silver plane swung low over Georgia Strait and lined up for the runway at Vancouver's airport. Molly, who was sitting by the window, suddenly pointed.

"Look," she said. "I think I can see Porlier Pass!"

The others craned their necks to catch a glimpse of the narrow pass between Galiano and Valdes Islands, which they had traversed at the beginning of their last adventure on the West Coast two years ago.

The plane settled its bulk down onto the runway with barely a bump, a testament to the flying skills of the pilot, Jim Richardson. The children were sitting at the front of a plane that was mostly carrying cargo, and had flown with Jim from Montreal where he had delivered mail and picked up goods bound for points west. The trip from Southampton to Vancouver, via ocean liner and airplane, had taken them a total of seven days. Their last trip to Canada had taken ten days, including four days on a train.

SADLY, NINETEEN-YEAR-OLD Ian Phillips, the oldest of the Phillips clan, was not joining the children on this epic journey to British Columbia. He had just graduated from the naval college at Dartmouth and was waiting for his first posting. There was no way he would be granted two months' leave to make the trip. He was now officially grown up. He was still interested in the adventure, though, and the others promised to send him lots of letters and postcards from Canada.

The last two years had seen all the children, not just Ian, grow and change and develop new interests. Fifteen-year-old Molly MacTavish had started flying lessons, using her share of the reward money for finding Brother XII's treasure. She was a natural, and her instructor was confident she would pass her flight exams and get her pilot licence when she turned sixteen.

Leticia MacTavish was growing out of the role of older sister's sidekick. Now thirteen years old, she was curious about the world and loved learning new things. Unlike Molly, Leticia didn't mind sitting still for hours in a classroom memorizing everything from the lifecycle of a frog to the English kings and queens going back to King Arthur. Someday she hoped to become a great scholar; she just didn't know what subject she would study yet.

Fourteen-year-old Mark MacTavish had a one-track mind (well, two-track if you counted his love of food). He knew his future would involve engines. He had spent many hours laying tracks for his model railway in the cellar at An Cuileann, building set pieces and running his trains with accompanying whistles and bells.

At fifteen and a half, Sophie Phillips was a very keen Girl Guide. Her uniform was almost completely covered with the badges she had earned. Her most prized ones were for First Aid and Cookery, but she had also earned some fairly obscure ones such as Commonwealth Knowledge, Child Nurse, and Embroideress. Because she was so naturally responsible (or, as Molly might put it, bossy), Sophie was always in charge of the younger children on their camping trips and other adventures. She made sure everyone brushed their teeth, bathed, and went to bed on time. She not only cooked their meals but also tended to their scrapes and bruises (and, on one memorable occasion, a gunshot wound) with her trusty first-aid kit. She used to do all the chores and all the cleaning up, too, but ever since their last trip to Canada, the other children had learned to pitch in and do their part to help. They had seen another side of Sophie on that trip—the side with the short temper! And they knew it would be better for everyone involved if they divided up the tasks from then on. Sophie now felt much more like an explorer and much less like a general dogsbody to the rest of the crew.

After she got home from Canada the last time, thirteen-year-old Harriet Phillips had written down the story of their adventures, illustrated with drawings and maps of their travels. Mr. and Mrs. Phillips had been so impressed with their daughter that they had had it printed and bound, and last Christmas everyone in the two families received a copy. Harriet loved drawing and writing, and she thought she might like to become a children's author and illustrator.

The youngest of the children, ten-year-old Posy Phillips, was now pony mad. She and her two sisters took riding lessons at school, but she was the only one who was passionate about horses. She spent every spare minute at the school stables, grooming the little bay Welsh pony that she took lessons on. His name was Whisky, as he was the colour of that famous Scottish drink. Even though Posy shared him with several other small girls, she thought of him as her pony. She had been begging her parents to buy her a pony of her own, but so far they had not relented. She wasn't giving up.

THE VOYAGE ACROSS the Atlantic by ocean liner had unfolded much like the last time. The children felt like seasoned transatlantic travellers, and although they enjoyed the voyage, they couldn't wait to get to Vancouver to find out what Captain Gunn had planned for them.

The flight across Canada took twenty hours, with several stops along the way. They left at 6:00 a.m. from Montreal and followed the sun westwards so that almost the entire flight was in daylight. The weather was mostly clear, and they were able to see endless rolling prairie, towering mountains, and eventually the clear blue waters of the Pacific Ocean. Molly spent a good portion of the flight sitting in the jump seat behind the captain, asking him loads of questions: What was the worst weather he had ever flown through? How old did you have to be to get a pilot's licence in Canada? What score had he gotten on his final flying exam? What did he think about female pilots? Did he believe Amelia Earhart was still alive somewhere? The poor pilot could barely concentrate on flying the plane while answering Molly's questions to her satisfaction. He was relieved when Mark insisted on taking Molly's place in the jump seat, but that relief didn't last long before Mark started in on his questions about the inner workings of the plane's engine!

At each stop, everyone disembarked onto the runway, and Sophie made the children stretch their legs, circle their arms, and do jumping jacks to get the kinks out.

"Gosh, anyone would think you were a gym teacher," quipped Leticia.

On one stretch between stops, Leticia tried to get everyone to look out the window and play I Spy, but the plane was moving so fast that it was impossible to keep the thing being "spied" in sight long enough for the others to guess what it was.

Meanwhile, Posy was rapidly growing bored, irritable, and tired. Sophie had come armed with Posy's favourite books, a sketchpad, and coloured pencils, but nothing seemed to draw the usually sweet little girl out of her foul mood.

"I know it's only taking one day to get to Vancouver instead of four days on the train, but flying is really, really boring," whined Posy, kicking the seat in front of her. "And noisy," she added, speaking loudly over the roar of the engines.

Sophie sighed, lamenting the fact that Girl Guides didn't have a badge for entertaining restless children on long plane trips. If only Posy could just sleep for the rest of the trip. Then suddenly she had an idea.

"Let's play...er...'Imagine,'" she said.

"'Imagine'?" Posy asked. "What's that?"

"It's a game where you close your eyes and imagine a scene in your head and then you... uh... describe certain details about it."

Posy looked at her sister as if she was crazy. That sounded more like a school assignment than a game.

"Now, why don't you close your eyes and imagine... er... I know! Imagine whole a row of ponies jumping over a fence."

Posy looked doubtfully at Sophie, but eventually obeyed because there was nothing else to do.

"Can you see the ponies?" Sophie asked.

"Yes, they all look just like Whisky!" Posy perked up, her eyes fluttering open.

"No, no, you must keep your eyes closed," Sophie warned. "Good. Now how many can you count?"

"One... two... three..." Posy began, her brow furrowed as she concentrated on the imaginary ponies.

"Good, good. Now keep counting them," Sophie said, amazed that her plan might actually work on a ten-year-old.

"... seven... eight..." Posy continued, her voice getting dreamy. By the time she reached "thirty-four" she was whispering, and her brow was smooth. By "sixty-two" she was fast asleep, her mind far away in pony-land.

Sophie breathed a sigh of relief and settled in for the remainder of the journey in peace.

Finally, and none to soon for everyone except Molly, the plane rolled to a stop outside the terminal building in

Vancouver. As soon as a set of steps had been pushed up to the plane's door, the children descended onto the runway, where Captain Gunn awaited them.

"Jolly glad to see you all!" he exclaimed as he greeted them. "Let's get your luggage and go to the hotel."

Dusk had finally given way to a velvety night, the lights of the airport competing with a blanket of stars and a sickle moon that had risen over the waters of Georgia Strait. The children were very tired, but the excitement of the arrival was enough to keep them awake as the taxi took them from the airport to the hotel.

Captain Gunn had stayed for several months at the Sylvia Hotel while writing his last book, which was inspired by the discovery of Brother XII's treasure. He had arrived back in Canada a couple of months earlier and settled into the same apartment he had occupied before. It wasn't the poshest of places, but it had the luxury of being located right across the street from the beach.

"You can't see much right now, but that's English Bay out there," said Captain Gunn when they and their luggage had finally made it up to the apartment. "Last time you were here, we sailed out of Burrard Inlet to your right, and headed across English Bay into Georgia Strait. The bridge you saw under construction is almost finished now, and it's a marvel. You have to hand it to those engineers!"

Posy had plopped onto the sofa and fallen asleep. Sophie covered her with a blanket and the rest of the crew collapsed onto their beds and were asleep in minutes.

"WAKEY, WAKEY, YOU lazybones," called Captain Gunn at 10:00 the next morning. "I didn't bring you halfway around the world to lie in bed!"

The children were soon washed and dressed and sitting around the breakfast table looking out over English Bay. The bay was dotted with sailboats, rowing boats, large ships heading into and out of Burrard Inlet, and any small vessel that could get its owners out on the brilliant blue waters. The children could feel a delicious warm breeze wafting in through the open window. The beach below was already busy with families setting up their spots for the day with deck chairs, umbrellas, picnic hampers, and children's toys. It looked a bit like an English seaside scene, except that no English resort had seemingly endless forests that climbed higher and higher towards the towering mountain peaks. The beach below them also boasted a pier and concrete bathhouse, with ice cream vendors manoeuvring for the best positions along the shore and a small herd of donkeys giving rides on the beach to the smaller children.

"We've got a wonderful day ahead," said Captain Gunn. "I think you should all go out and spend some time on the beach and then later we are meeting up with some old friends for a picnic. Actually, they call them barbeques here, so we'd better get with the lingo! We are going to cook one of your favourite Canadian delicacies, hamburgers, on the grill."

"Who's coming?" asked Harriet.

"Let me see," said Captain Gunn pulling a crumpled piece of paper out of his pocket. "There's Joe, our old friend from

DeCourcy Island, and his wife, Maggie, who you will be glad to hear is now living at home again. It took a bit a persuading, but Jasper Peabody has come down from Mink Island, and Pete the Mountie will be here, too. I've invited Mr. Schroeder from the Hotel Vancouver and Mr. Goldstein, our lawyer. Hope they can both make it. Oh, and Jim Spilsbury is flying down from Savary Island. It should be quite a party!"

The children quickly changed into their bathing suits, grabbed some towels, and headed down to the beach where they found a spot to leave their shoes and towels before racing down to the water.

"Ow, it's freezing," shrieked Molly, who had been the first to plunge into the water.

The others hesitated, but they were all intrepid explorers, and a bit of cold water wasn't going to stop them. Soon they were all swimming and playing, and the air was so warm that they quickly forgot the initial shock of jumping into the Pacific Ocean.

Captain Gunn was comfortably ensconced in a deck chair on the beach, with his hat tipped over his nose and his feet bare. The children joined him, shivering and jumping up and down, and he gave a tremendous whistle to summon the nearest ice cream seller.

"Not sure if ice cream is the right thing to warm you up, but I'm sure you all remember how delicious Canadian ices are."

Sitting on the sand in the full sun with their huge cones, they were warm again in no time.

LATER THAT AFTERNOON the whole crew headed towards Stanley Park, a short walk away along the beachfront road. In some ways the park resembled those they knew in England, complete with bowling green, lawns, flowerbeds, and paths winding here and there, but it also had the element of wilderness that they had first experienced on their last visit to Canada. The lawns and flowerbeds made way in the distance to dense forest, but their destination was close to the beach with a picnic area and firepits. As guests arrived, everyone started sharing stories from their previous adventures and catching up on the news of the past two years.

The previous Christmas Leticia had received a Kodak Brownie camera and had taken a couple of rolls of practice film before leaving on their trip. She felt confident enough to line everyone up and take a couple of shots. She even asked a passer by to take a third one with her in the group, and she hoped that one would turn out all right when she had the film developed. She was determined to document their adventures and make an album when she got home.

It was a wonderful evening that only ended when Sophie noticed that all the younger members of the party were yawning. It had been a very busy couple of days and they were suddenly extremely tired. The children left the grown-ups still chatting around the campfire and walked back to the hotel, where they fell into their beds. Just before she fell asleep, Molly sat bolt upright.

"We still don't know what Uncle Bert has planned for us," she said.

"Don't worry," replied Leticia. "He's bound to have something good up his sleeve. He's never let us down yet."

THE NEXT MORNING after the crew had finished their hearty Canadian breakfast, and after Captain Gunn had filled and lit his pipe, he leaned back in his chair and spilled the beans.

"Some of you might be sorry to hear this, but we are going to turn our backs on the ocean for the time being and embark on an entirely new adventure."

Molly glanced out of the window at the enticing view of ocean and the dozens of sailboats out in the bay taking advantage of the summer weather, and looked her uncle square in the eye.

"You know that I am a sailor at heart, Uncle Bert, but even sailors have to spend time ashore, and I think you must have something pretty exciting up your sleeve."

Captain Gunn eyed his niece and chuckled.

"Very diplomatic, my dear," he said, "and you are quite right, I do have a pretty exciting adventure planned. And I don't think any of you could have guessed what it is in a hundred years! You all know about my books. Well, it seems my readers can't get enough, and I've been racking my brains trying to come up with something interesting enough to tempt my publisher. Actually, I didn't really need to tempt them. They were very relieved that I had another idea since they are making a lot of money off me. So," and here he paused.

"Don't tease us," said Leticia. "Come on, out with it."

Captain Gunn sat forward in his chair and continued.

"All of you would be forgiven in thinking that the age of the cowboy has been left behind, along with gun slinging and other activities associated with the Wild West. You'd be mistaken, however, because the cowboy is alive and well and living in the Interior of British Columbia. There are some massive ranches up there, some as big as entire counties in England, and they run thousands of cattle. Those hamburgers you devoured last night probably started life on one of those ranches. One of the biggest is the Douglas Lake Ranch near Merritt, and I've been corresponding with them.

"My next book is going to be a history of cattle ranching and the modern cowboy. I'm also very interested in how they move hundreds of cattle from one spot to another and so have arranged for us all to accompany a herd of cattle from Merritt over to the Okanagan Lake. We," and here he glanced round at the children's faces, "are going to go on a mounted cattle drive, complete with cowboy camping and cookouts!"

Posy had turned several shades of pink and her eyes sparkled as she realized that of all the children, she knew the most about horses. The youngest she might be, but she could beat Molly hands down on any quiz about riding or horse care.

Captain Gunn read her thoughts and turned to the rest of the crew.

"We happen to have our own horse expert as part of our crew, so Posy is going to take on the role of horse master in our group. I don't think anyone," and here he glanced sternly at Molly, "can second guess her when it comes to matters of the horse."

Posy was ecstatic. Finally she had become a valuable member of the crew, and not just the baby along for the ride. She couldn't wait.

"What about the rest of you who can't ride as well as I can?" she said.

"Everyone, and that includes me, is going to take riding lessons for a few days before we leave on the cattle drive. We are going to stay at the Quilchena Hotel, which is near the Douglas Lake Ranch and where they have horses and cattle of their own which are going to join the drive. Not sure how I'll manage, or even if they can find a horse that won't collapse under me, but they've assured me that they have a large selection of horses. We'll all be assigned one and will care for it and take lessons on it during our stay."

The crew all started chattering and asking questions, but Captain Gunn had said all he was going to say about the upcoming adventure.

"Tomorrow we are going to take the train to Nicola, which is just outside of Merritt. Today I'd like Sophie to supervise repacking your bags. You can leave anything associated with fancy dinners and parties behind, and just take shorts and shirts and one sweater each. I've heard it can get cool in the evenings, although you will have to prepare yourselves for some pretty extreme heat during the day. The climate in the Interior is quite different from what you have experienced on the coast. This afternoon we are all going to go downtown and fix everyone up with a pair of blue jeans, suitable for riding. The Quilchena Hotel has a general store attached and they've assured me that we can get kitted out with boots and hats there."

THAT AFTERNOON THE whole party boarded the streetcar that took them downtown to the Army and Navy store. It was chock-full of fascinating stuff, especially in the camping department, but Captain Gunn assured them that the hotel would be able to supply them with all the camping gear they and the cowboys would need. They were solely shopping for blue jeans.

They had only ever seen jeans in the cowboy movies they had occasionally watched, so they were all excited about having a pair of their own. One thing was certain: they would be the only children back home who owned genuine blue jeans. The store had a huge display in all sizes, and eventually they were able to find ones to fit everyone. Sophie guessed at Ian's size so they could take a pair back to England for him. Captain Gunn posed a bit of a problem, as he was distinctly lacking in a waist, so any pair big enough was in danger of falling down. He solved this problem by buying a bright red pair of logger's suspenders, which when attached to the jeans kept them in the spot where his waist would have been, had he had one. He couldn't resist the colourful checked loggers' shirts and bought one each for the children in the smallest sizes available, but unfortunately they didn't come in children's sizes, so Posy and Harriet (who was small for her age) had to do without. Captain Gunn also bought a small duffel bag for each of them.

Back at the hotel Sophie supervised the repacking and soon their baggage was reduced to fit into their new duffel bags. Molly was delighted to be leaving the frocks behind that her mother had once again insisted on them packing. All the girls had worn dresses every evening for dinner on the ocean liner, but now there would be no need for them. Cowboys, or even children accompanying cowboys, had no need of pretty frocks. The hotel would store the rest of their luggage until they returned to Vancouver.

"Don't forget to pack your toothbrushes and hair brushes," Sophie reminded everyone. "I'll take one tin of toothpowder for us all to share and I have a big bar of soap in a case."

The bags were piled neatly by the door, and after an early supper and a quick walk down to the beach, Sophie ushered everyone off to bed.

"It looks like we'll have a long day tomorrow, and we want to be rested so that we don't fall asleep on the train and miss anything."

No one could argue with that sentiment, and with the curtains drawn against the long evening of light, the crew settled down for a good sleep. Soon the apartment resonated to the gentle sound of Captain Gunn's snores.

CHAPTER TWO
LEAVING THE COAST BEHIND

Early the next morning, the six children and Captain Gunn once again boarded the streetcar to the train station.

After buying tickets, Captain Gunn led them to the platform where their train stood quietly puffing steam as it readied itself for departure. The train they were boarding was not the huge transcontinental that on their last trip had brought them all the way from Montreal to Vancouver, but a much smaller one that would be making several stops before arriving in Hope, at the head of the Fraser Valley.

They settled themselves in a carriage, and soon the train steamed its way out of the station, with Burrard Inlet clearly visible to their left. The train wound its way through the Vancouver suburbs and then headed east through cultivated farmland, interspersed with patches of forest. The ever-present mountains hemmed the valley as well as presenting what appeared to be an impenetrable barrier ahead.

"Gosh, what's that mountain?" asked Harriet pointing out of the right side of the carriage.

A massive snowcapped peak reared itself higher than any of the other mountains, and appeared to be an almost perfect cone.

"Here, let's take a look at the map," said Captain Gunn, spreading a large sheet across the carriage. "This map shows the whole of British Columbia and some of Washington State. See who can find that mountain first on the map."

Everyone craned their necks for a good view, but it was Harriet, with her experience in drawing maps of her own, that figured it out first.

"It's called Mount Baker," she said triumphantly.

"Yes, you're right," said Captain Gunn, "and I think from the look of it, it's an extinct volcano. Although perhaps not entirely extinct! We are in a very active earthquake zone here and earthquakes and volcanoes are often found in the same places."

Posy looked a little worried. She remembered the earthquake they had experienced on their last trip, and really wasn't that keen on being around for the next one.

"I shouldn't worry," said Captain Gunn, noticing her face. "We are heading up into the Interior of British Columbia where earthquakes are pretty much unheard of."

The train followed the course of the mighty Fraser River and, after making several stops along the way to drop off and pick up passengers, huffed its way into the small town of Hope. Collecting their possessions they descended from the train, which quickly departed on its journey up the Fraser Canyon.

Captain Gunn consulted with the man in the ticket booth and returned with a fistful of tickets.

"We have an hour to wait before our train on the Kettle Valley Railway up to Merritt leaves, and I see just where I'm going to spend it," he said, ambling over to a shade-covered bench.

"Well, I think we can count Captain Gunn out for any exploring," laughed his younger niece. "Let's take a look around."

"Just make sure you're back at least fifteen minutes before the train is due to leave," said Captain Gunn, now comfortably relaxing on his bench as he prepared to light up his pipe.

The children walked out of the station and looked around. Hope appeared to be a sleepy little town in a magnificent setting. In front of them was the Fraser River, slow moving at this time of the year as it meandered and threaded its way between shoals of gravel on its way westwards towards the Pacific Ocean.

On each side of the river, hills formed walls to the valley, which they could see flattening out in the distance. Behind them, however, massive peaks appeared to completely block the way east.

Harriet noticed a board on the wall of the station and went over to take a look.

"That's interesting," she said. "This board tells a little about the history of the Kettle Valley Railway." The others gathered round and she read from the board, pushing Mark out of the way as he blocked her view of the sign.

"'The KVR was the work of Andrew McCulloch, Chief Engineer for the Canadian Pacific Railway's new line in the southern interior of British Columbia—the Kettle Valley Railway. He was hired to build the railway when the fear of our

American neighbours exploiting BC's mineral wealth reached its peak. The result was the building of 325 miles of rail over and through three mountain ranges.'"

Mark, eager to take in any piece of train information before anyone else, took over reading:

"'The Kettle Valley Railway, including the Co... Coquihalla section,'" he began, struggling with the pronunciation of the strange new word, "'was completed in 1916. The thirty-nine-mile section from Coquihalla Summit to the CPR junction near Hope needed forty-three bridges, thirteen tunnels, and sixteen snow sheds. Construction crews used 22 million board feet of timber and 4,500 tons of steel. The entire railway cost almost $20 million, and took nearly twenty years to complete.'

"Gosh, that's amazing," said Mark, beaming at the others, who seemed to have lost interest while he was reading. "It certainly makes our English trains seem pretty tame."

No one seemed as excited as Mark until Molly said, "Let's see if we can find some ice cream!"

Twenty minutes later they were back at the station with their cones. Mark lingered by the sign, marvelling at the incredible feat of building the railway. The others wandered up the platform, where Captain Gunn was fast asleep on his bench. They found another bench so they wouldn't disturb him and sat down to wait for the train.

About ten minutes later it entered the station with a whistle, startling Captain Gunn out of his nap.

"Everyone, grab your luggage and queue up in a straight line!" ordered Sophie in her bossiest teacher-voice. "You too, Captain Gunn!"

The group scrambled to locate the correct bags, which were all in a pile next to the bench where Captain Gunn had been sleeping. Leticia grabbed Harriet's bag by mistake, and Harriet began to panic when she discovered her bag was "missing." By the time Sophie figured out the mix-up, the conductor was already calling "All aboooooard!" and there was no time to line up.

Captain Gunn took charge and lifted each child (and their luggage) up off the platform and gave them a little toss onto the train. Sophie and Molly were too big to be tossed, so they quickly skipped up the steps of the train. Captain Gunn grabbed his bag and one other that no one had claimed and lumbered up the steps and into the carriage.

"You see, Sophie?" Captain Gunn boomed, as the train pulled out of the station. "Sometimes there's no time for fussing about with queues. Sometimes you just have to take charge and..."

"Wait, Captain Gunn," she said, alarm rising in her voice. "Just wait a minute." She started doing a head-count, putting a hand on each child's head as she went. Then suddenly she sucked in her breath.

"For heaven's sake, Sophie! You're white as a sheet! Whatever is the ma—"

"M-M-MARK!" Sophie wailed, covering her mouth with her hands, so it came out more like, "MMM-AAAGH!"

"What?"

"Huh?"

The other children and Captain Gunn looked at each other, bewildered.

Just then, Leticia exclaimed, "Golly! Where's Mark?"

Sophie made another indecipherable sound.

Captain Gunn yelled out a word not usually heard in polite company.

Molly, gleeful that the adventure was starting so early in their trip, declared, "I'll go find the conductor and order him to stop the train!"

But as it turned out, that wasn't necessary because just then they heard an adolescent voice yelling, "Waaaaiit!"

They all crowded to the window and saw Mark running desperately along the platform, looking wildly towards the train as if a door would magically open and suck him inside. It seemed hopeless until, apparently from nowhere, three men appeared. Two of them caught up with Mark, grabbed an elbow each, and practically lifted Mark off his feet.

"Quick, open your door," one of them panted.

Molly ran to the door and flung it open, and the two men threw Mark through the door and onto the floor of the carriage.

"You young idiot," said Captain Gunn. "You'd have been sitting on that platform until this time tomorrow if those men hadn't come along."

"Sorry, Uncle Bert," gasped Mark.

"I hope you didn't make those men miss the train," said Harriet.

They all leaned out of the windows and looked back along the platform.

"Oh, no! They've missed the carriage—it's only freight cars at the back of the train," said Molly, who had leaned out the farthest.

Captain Gunn pushed her aside and had a look for himself.

The three men disappeared as the train moved forward, and no one could see if they had jumped into a freight car or just got left behind.

"I don't think those are paying passengers. Unless I'm very much mistaken, those fellows are hopping a freight car for a free ride. Times have been hard over the last few years, and 'riding the rail cars' without paying the fare is very common."

"Hopping on board without paying?" Harriet exclaimed. "But that's like stealing! The rest of us have to pay. Why shouldn't those men?"

"Our parents are the ones paying, not us," said Sophie, who had just barely recovered from nearly losing Mark. "And I think Captain Gunn means those men are too poor to pay. I read in the newspaper on the ship coming over here that a lot of men are out of work in Canada. They ride the rails in the hopes of finding work in some other town. Often they go from town to town and barely make enough money to survive."

Everyone was silent as they pondered that thought. The children had occasionally seen poor people back home, especially when they made trips to London and other big cities. And they were always encouraged to give small donations to the poor out of their pocket money at Christmas and Easter. But the truth was, the closest they had ever come to poverty was from reading Charles Dickens novels. Seeing it firsthand, and knowing that these men were in the same boat as thousands of others, made it seem more real.

THE SEATS IN their train resembled park benches. There was only one carriage, the other part of the train being freight cars. As the train pulled out of the station, the guard came through the carriage checking tickets.

"You'll need to change trains again in Merritt," he said. "Just walk a little way up the track until you pass the junction, and the train to Nicola will be waiting for you. I was talking to the manager of the Quilchena Hotel this morning as he was delivering departing guests to the train, and he mentioned that he was expecting a party coming up from Vancouver. He'll have the wagon waiting for you at the station."

Captain Gunn thanked the guard for the instructions, and the children smiled politely, but the whole time they were thinking about the men they had seen. If they had successfully hopped aboard, what would happen to them if they got caught?

The train gathered speed as it left Hope behind and aimed itself straight at a massive mountain range. Nobody could see a way through, but the train kept going, following the course of the rushing river in the valley bottom; diving into tunnels and crossing and re-crossing the river on massive wooden trestles as they climbed higher and higher. The walls of the valley rose steep and sheer, with snow capped peaks towering above them.

It was the most unlikely place for a train to run, but run it did, stopping every so often at halts along the way for people to get on or off—although why anyone would be coming or going anywhere in this wilderness was a mystery to the children. The stops all had signs with names such as Portia, Romeo, and Juliet. Whoever had named them must have had a love of Mr. Shakespeare. The stops served another function as they all had water towers from which the steam engine filled its tanks. It was taking a tremendous amount of power to pull the train up the steep slope.

Finally, the grade levelled off, the train appeared to turn a corner, and the scenery abruptly changed from mountainous terrain to more gently rounded hills. A scent of pine wafted in through the open window and the air suddenly seemed warmer. What an extraordinary country this was! It was as if they had crossed a border into a different place altogether.

After following a relatively level plateau the train began to descend. Mark knew that it was almost as hard for a train to go downhill as it was to go uphill.

"If the brakes fail, we'll end up roaring down the hill and the driver won't be able to stop the train in Merritt," said Mark, looking slyly at his younger sister, whom he knew to be a bit of a scaredy cat.

The colour drained from Letitia's face and her lower lip began to tremble.

Captain Gunn gave Mark a stern glance and reassured Leticia that a brake failure was most unlikely. Of course, the train had no trouble and was soon pulling into the station at Merritt.

As they climbed down onto the platform with all their luggage, they glanced back and saw the three men from the train platform in Hope jumping out of a freight car attached to the train behind the passenger car. They looked a lot like the cowboys the children had occasionally seen in movies back home. They were all clad in grubby blue jeans, checked shirts, pointed boots, and cowboy hats. They followed Captain Gunn and the children as they walked out of the station and a little way up the track, as directed by the guard. It seemed that they too were bound for Nicola.

It was blazing hot. The sky was a clear pale blue and there was not a breath of breeze to give some relief from the heat. Fortunately they didn't have to walk far, and the little local train was waiting for them. They climbed aboard for the short trip up the line to Nicola.

The cowboys seemed to be travelling legitimately this time and joined them in the carriage. However, they weren't very talkative and sat in a silent group at the other end of the carriage. Molly glanced at them, taking particular note of the youngest in the group. Something about him seemed vaguely familiar. She tried to get a better look at him, but he had seated himself with his back to her and the others and tipped his hat down over his face.

It seemed no time at all before the train was stopping once more, and this time they had reached the end of a train journey as exciting, in its own way, as the cross Canada one they had taken two years before.

There was no proper station, just a gravelled area beside the track, with a dirt road leading off it. Parked on the gravel was a wagon pulled by two black horses, a cowboy sitting on the driver's seat. He hopped down and greeted them. He was tall, with an imposing handlebar moustache, a wide leather belt with a huge silver buckle, and elaborately stitched cowboy boots.

"Howdy!" he said. "I'm Sam Steele, chief horse wrangler and cow boss at the Quilchena. I'll be fixing you up with horses tomorrow and giving you your riding lessons. And you must be Posy," he said to the youngest member of the group who was patting and talking to the horses. "I've heard all about you. I won't have to teach you too much about riding and horse care, or so I've been led to believe!"

Posy turned bright pink and smiled shyly.

"How'd you like to ride up front with me," said Sam. "The rest of you will have to pile in the back with your luggage."

Posy climbed up on the driver's seat alongside Sam and the others loaded themselves and their luggage into the back. Captain Gunn was already suffering in the heat. His face had turned beet red and he was mopping at his forehead with his handkerchief.

As the wagon pulled away Harriet glanced back.

"It looks like the cowboys have to walk," she said. "They're going to get awfully hot."

"Don't worry about them," said Sam from the driver's seat. "The heat won't bother them, those guys are tough. Someone will probably give them a lift, at least part of the way."

The cowboys had slung their bags over their shoulders as they started to walk. They were soon left behind as the horses broke into a trot and the wagon sped up.

Their route took them through a small settlement with some houses, a church, and a school.

"This is Nicola," said Sam. "Some of the permanent crew have families and live here. The casual cowboys, like that bunch that got off the train with you, stay in the bunkhouses behind the hotel."

Soon the village was left behind and the road headed into open country. The scenery was completely different from anything they had seen on the coast. Gone were the towering mountains and thick forests. Here there were rolling hills covered with yellow grass and the occasional stand of pine trees. It was very, very hot and the children were thirsty and felt dusty and dirty. The journey had been long and they were all tired. And then they all perked up, because appearing on their left was the beginning of a lake that stretched up the valley as far as they could see. Visions of a cool dip in the lake danced before their eyes.

The wagon moved briskly along the road beside the lake and soon they were turning in to the gravelled area in front of the hotel.

The Quilchena Hotel stood four square and massive, three storeys high with a wide double-storey veranda on the front.

Apart from the buildings of downtown Vancouver, this was by far the largest house the children had seen on their Canadian adventures.

Sam pulled the wagon to a halt by the front steps, and a couple came out to greet them.

The man was small and neat, and looked the exact opposite of Sam. No jeans here; he was wearing a white shirt and tie with crisply pressed black trousers. The woman wore a floral dress covered in a snowy white apron and looked kind and welcoming.

"Hi there," said the man. "I'm Arnold Schwimmer, and this is my wife, Rose. We manage the hotel and we're mighty glad that you made the journey safely. Come along. Sam can give you a hand with your bags, and Rose will show you to your rooms. Dinner will be ready in an hour. I'll see you then." And with that he disappeared round the back of the building, leaving Rose and Sam to help them inside.

Inside the hotel they glanced at a huge parlour to their left and a dining room to the right. Straight ahead was an impressive staircase that rose to the upper floors. Rose led the way, the children and Captain Gunn followed, and Sam brought up the rear with some of their luggage.

On the second storey Rose led them along a wide corridor, opening doors to right and left.

"I've put Sophie, Harriet, and Posy in this nice big room with Molly and Leticia next door. There's a bathroom down the hall on the right and another one at the other end of the hall."

Rose had obviously done her homework and read the letter from Captain Gunn that described the requirements of the group.

"Mr. Cameron," (that was Captain Gunn), "I've given you a room facing the lake so you'll get a nice breeze. And for Mark we've got a small room at the very end of the hall. Oh, and we don't have electricity in the house, so I'll show you later how to manage the oil lamps in your rooms. The days are long right now, so you won't need them until later this evening. We're all used to it, but some of our guests think we are very old-fashioned!"

Harriet was actually thrilled by the novelty of using oil lamps in an historic old hotel. It really was like something out of a Wild West movie.

After the extreme heat of the outdoors, it was relatively cool inside the hotel. The high ceilings helped, as did the slowly moving fans in the hallways and each of the rooms. (Rose told them later that the fans ran on huge batteries that were charged every so often by a diesel-powered generator.)

Once everyone found the right luggage, Sophie took over.

"We're all dusty and dirty, and I think we should all go to our rooms and take a nice cool bath before dinner. Looking at that dining room, I'm sorry we left all our good clothes in Vancouver—Molly, I can see you rolling your eyes!—but everyone find your nicest shorts and clean shirts and make sure your hair is brushed for dinner. You too, Captain Gunn!"

Giving orders about domestic matters was second nature to Sophie. Often she felt more like a mother than an older sister or friend, which was especially ridiculous when she had to order Molly around. Not that Molly was one to follow directions. The two girls were practically the same age, but they couldn't have been more different in temperament.

"Honestly, Sophie," Molly said with a grin that was not entirely kind, "sometimes I think you'd be happier if we all sat round embroidering cushion covers in our best party frocks!"

Sophie gave Molly a haughty look, but the comment had stung. She secretly hated being thought of as prissy. Just because she was good at cooking and cleaning and keeping things orderly didn't mean she was a goody-two-shoes.

"Don't be mean," piped up Leticia in Sophie's defence. "You know as well as I do that Mother and Mrs. Phillips wouldn't let us do half the things we do if it weren't for Sophie being so organized and practical."

Captain Gunn gave Molly a stern look. "Remember that without Sophie our expeditions would be a lot less comfortable. We all know you are an intrepid pirate, but even pirates needed clean clothes and hot meals, so button up and give your friend some respect."

Sophie gave Leticia and Captain Gunn a grateful smile and avoided eye contact with Molly as she ushered the rest of the children upstairs.

Captain Gunn had his own bathroom, and the others took turns in the two bathrooms on their floor. Each contained a massive claw-foot bathtub and marble-topped sink as well as a lavatory built like a throne.

An hour later the crew descended the staircase and found their way into the parlour, where Captain Gunn was already sitting by the open window with a glass of whisky. They were the only children, though several other guests sat in the parlour, drinks in hand.

"Take a look in the bar next door," he said, waving his glass towards another door in the corner.

The bar was massive, its wooden surfaces polished to a shine, a brass foot rail along the bottom and bar stools lined up along the front. Mr. Schwimmer was standing behind it shining glasses and serving beer to a couple of cowboys who leaned up against it. The children recognized them as the two men who had thrown Mark on the train. Mark went over and thanked them and they responded with huge grins.

"No problem, kid!," said one before returning to his beer.

"Take a look down there," said Mr. Schwimmer, pointing to the front of the bar. "Can you see the bullet holes?"

"Gosh, we really are in the Wild West," said Molly, glancing at the cowboys to see if they were carrying guns.

Mr. Schwimmer noticed her looking and reassured them.

"Those holes were shot back in 1910, when a couple of drunk cowboys were cut off from being served any more liquor. Don't worry, our boys are much better behaved these days and only carry shotguns out on the range. Now, I've got lemonade or cola, which would you like?"

The children all chose cola and took their drinks back into the parlour with Captain Gunn. They had developed a taste for the fizzy drink on their last trip to Canada and couldn't wait to get their hands on the ice-cold bottles.

"Now," he said, "I'm going to fill you in on our plans for the next couple of days. Tomorrow we are going to start our riding lessons with Sam. So I want everyone down for breakfast at 7:30. It's best to get out there early before it gets really hot. You will each be assigned a horse, and we'll have a lesson each day until we start on our cattle drive. In the afternoons I'm going to do some research—they have lots of books full of cuttings and photographs, which will be a great help with writing my book. Oh, and I'll need a nice long nap too. Jolly exhausting in this heat. You can walk down to the lake after lunch if you like. You'll enjoy a swim after mornings spent around the horses. By the way, I have a bit of a surprise for you, but you'll have to wait a few days, and it will depend on how you do with your riding lessons. It's no good looking at me like that, Molly, I'm as good at keeping secrets as you are at dreaming up the next escapade!"

It was about as different from their last trip as could be, but even Molly was beginning to see the possibilities of an adventure in cowboy country.

They all moved into the dining room with the other guests, and Rose served up a delicious dinner of roast beef and apple pie.

"You won't find a better piece of beef anywhere this side of the Rocky Mountains," said Rose. "This time last week it was roaming the range!"

Posy wasn't sure how she felt about such a personal connection to her dinner, but after one bite she agreed that the beef was delicious.

"The happier the cow's life is, the better the taste of its meat," added Rose and everyone thought it was the best roast beef they had ever tasted. It was certainly a far cry from the sad, thin slices of roast beef served at the girls' boarding school or even the Sunday roasts at home, where the beef was the minor part of a meal that included potatoes, Yorkshire pudding, two veg, and gravy. Here the thick juicy slices of beef took pride of place, and soon everyone's plates were wiped clean.

It wasn't long before everyone was yawning over their dishes of apple pie and thanking Rose. They left Captain Gunn with his post-dinner cigar and whisky and headed upstairs for a good night's sleep.

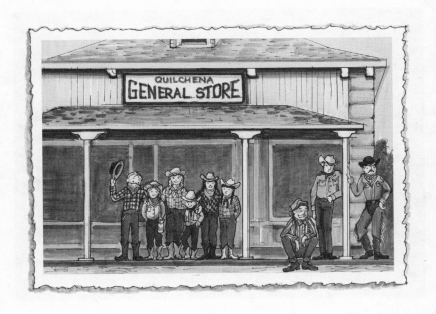

CHAPTER THREE

RIDE 'EM, COWBOYS AND COWGIRLS!

The next morning they were all up and dressed in plenty of time for breakfast, wearing their brand new blue jeans in anticipation of their riding lessons. They had a little time to explore the hotel and discovered a side door that led directly into the bar, with a hitching rail outside for the horses of cowboys who needed a drink. The hotel was surrounded by green lawns, obviously kept watered, as everything else was bone dry and brown. A small stream appeared to come from the hills behind the hotel and wound its way towards the lake. It was edged with several large willow trees. The hotel also boasted some well-kept rose beds, and there were deck chairs set out in the shade under the willows. It was a lovely spot.

Just as they were finishing breakfast in the dining room, Sam appeared at the door.

"You've got time to visit the store and sort out some boots and hats; then it will be time to saddle up," he said. "Good idea to beat the heat and do your riding early in the morning."

Everyone trooped out and over to the store, which was close to the hotel and faced the road. The building had three sides of wood and one of stone. There was a porch along the front and three horses were already tied up at the hitching rail. Clearly, this was where the cowboys did their shopping.

Inside, the store was filled with everything an aspiring cowboy or cowgirl could need. Hats, boots, jeans, saddlebags, even saddles and bridles—some of them studded with silver. The establishment also served as a general store for the surrounding area and stocked a wide variety of goods. Sacks of flour and beans, canned goods, cooking utensils, bolts of fabric, kerosene, coffee, and jars of stick candy jostled for space, many items hanging from hooks on the ceiling. In the middle of it all was a large pot-bellied stove.

"No time to explore right now," said Captain Gunn. "You can come back later after your riding lessons if you like. For now we are on a quest for boots and hats."

A young woman in blue jeans and a checked shirt came forward to help the children, and soon they were all kitted out in some of the plainer of the cowboy boots and straw cowboy hats designed to keep the worst of the heat off their faces. She was even able to find boots to fit Posy. As she explained, the hotel had many young visitors who, even if they didn't go riding, wanted some cowboy gear to take home as souvenirs. Captain Gunn noticed a pile of brightly patterned silk kerchiefs and added one each to the pile.

"Keep these knotted round your necks to help to soak up the sweat," he said. "I have a feeling that I'll be needing mine more than anyone!"

Quickly putting their old shoes in a neat line on the back porch and wearing their new boots, everyone walked around the back of the hotel and towards a large barn surrounded by fenced corrals. Standing in one of the corrals were seven horses, ranging from a pony to one that resembled a carthorse.

"Your uncle sent me details of your size and riding experience," said Sam after he'd admired their new gear, "so I've pulled these ones out of the remuda and we'll see how you do."

"What's a remuda?" asked Posy, who was constantly adding to her store of horsy terminology.

"That's the name we give to our herd of horses," said Sam. "It's a Spanish word meaning 'change of horses.' The cowboys pick their horses from the remuda and the person in charge of the remuda is generally known as the head wrangler; that's me. I'm the cow boss, too, so I'm a busy guy!"

The group stood around the corral, and Sam went in with a handful of halters. The first horse he picked was the smallest. It was white splashed with black spots and had a white mane and a black tail. It didn't look like any pony Posy had ever seen.

"This little fellow is for you, Posy," he said. "His name is Spotty, and I believe he was bred from an Appaloosa/Arab crossed with a Shetland pony. He's a great little horse and a favourite with some of our regular young visitors. I only assign him to good riders because he can be a bit of a handful, but I'm sure you will manage him just fine."

Posy gazed entranced between the rails of the corral. It was love at first sight. At last she was going to have her very own pony that she didn't have to share with anyone else. And what an extraordinary animal he was!

Sam haltered Spotty up, opened the gate, and handed the lead rope to Posy.

"Take him over to the barn and tie him to the hitching rail. Ask one of the cowboys to find you a bucket of brushes."

Sam turned and looked at the rest of the group.

"We'll fix up Sophie and Harriet next," he said. "I know you have done a bit of riding at school, so you're not total beginners. I've got the perfect pair for you."

Back in the corral he selected a pair of horses with similar colouring that were a bit bigger than Posy's.

"These are buckskin quarter horses. Bred specifically for ranch work and got lots of experience. This one's Sonny, and this one's Jake."

Jake was a bright coffee colour with a black mane and tail, and Sonny was a bit darker with two white socks on his hind legs. Sophie and Harriet took the lead ropes and went over to join Posy at the hitching rail.

"Now the rest of you were a bit harder to match with suitable horses," said Sam. "I had to ask around and found these three at the neighbouring ranch. They've been used in rodeos as parade horses, so they are bomb-proof. You should do fine."

"What does he mean, 'bomb-proof'?" Leticia whispered nervously to Molly.

"Shhh..." said Molly, rather than admit that she didn't know—and possibly betray the fact that she was pretty nervous herself.

Sam led out three horses, one brown and white, one black and white, and one with a mottled reddish coat.

"Those coloured horses are paints and the other one is an Appaloosa. Great horses, all of them. Jigsaw, Mappie, and Strawberry," he added, pointing to the horses in turn.

Molly, Leticia, and Mark rather tentatively took their horses and headed over to the barn. Horses were definitely not their cup of tea.

That left Captain Gunn. The only remaining horse in the corral—with a white strip down its face and hairy black feet—was obviously for him. It resembled one of the horses used to pull milk floats and small farm wagons.

Sam looked doubtfully at his last and biggest student.

"We'll have to see how you get on, but if all else fails you can always ride on the wagon with the rest of the gear. This old fellow is steady as a rock. In fact, his name is Rocky."

Captain Gunn couldn't face being relegated to the wagon like a sack of flour or a case of beans. He was going to learn to ride—although he was going to need a stepladder to heave himself into the saddle.

He and Sam headed over to join the others at the barn. Sam whistled, and a couple of cowboys emerged from the dim and dusty barn carrying a load of tack. The children recognized them as two of the train-hopping cowboys, the same ones who had been drinking at the bar the day before.

"Gerry and Joey here are going to show you how to tack up. After today you're on your own, but they'll be here to give you a hand if you get stuck. Make sure your horse is brushed well, especially the bits where the saddle and girth go. Best way to get a saddle-sore horse is for its tack to go on over mud and dirt."

The saddles were large and heavy with a horn at the front and massive stirrups. The younger members of the party needed help to lift them onto the horses' backs. Gerry and Joey showed them how the girths did up without any buckles, just by threading them back and forth through a large ring under the saddle flap, and then showed them how to put on the bridles. Posy didn't like the look of the bits, which were not the gentle snaffles used on the ponies back in England. She resolved never to yank on Spotty's mouth.

When everyone was ready, Sam led them into a big corral, which, to Captain Gunn's relief, had a mounting block in the corner.

"This is where we teach the young cowboys to ride," said Sam, "and where we break the young horses. We've had some rodeos in here, I can tell you!"

Everyone mounted and Sam stood in the middle as they walked around. The saddles felt very odd, but they also felt as if it would be hard to fall out of them. Captain Gunn looked funny with his bright red suspenders, gaily patterned kerchief knotted around his neck, and large cowboy hat. He could have won a contest as an Englishman's version of a Wild West cowboy.

Posy led the line of horses going round the ring, and soon Sam had them all walking and halting on command. Things went downhill when they were instructed to kick their horses into a trot. Of course that was no problem for Posy, once she got the hang of sitting to the trot like a cowboy, and not trying to do the elegant rising trot she was used to. The others, however, were flopping around, hanging onto the horns of their saddles and generally trying hard not to fall off.

Molly—who was used to being the best at every outdoor activity she tried—was starting to resent Jigsaw for having a mind of his own. When she started daydreaming about sailing on the lake, her distraction gave Jigsaw an excuse to take a quick sideways step and deposit Molly in the dust.

"Ouch," she said ruefully, rubbing her rear end and glaring at Leticia and Mark for giggling at her misfortune.

"Molly, you'd better get back up on Jigsaw and go round the ring once more, or he'll think he's got away with dumping you," said Sam. "After that, I think you've all had enough for today." This came as a relief to everyone except Posy. "You only have a week to learn how to ride well enough to join in the cattle drive, so first thing tomorrow morning you can collect your horses and tack up and be ready for your lesson at 9:00."

AFTER LUNCH CAPTAIN Gunn settled himself in the parlour with a stack of books and albums of old photographs. The others headed upstairs to change into their swimming gear. The lake beckoned, and they couldn't wait to cool off. As they headed out the front door, Molly glanced into the parlour.

"Doesn't look like Uncle Bert is doing much research," she laughed.

And indeed Captain Gunn was relaxing in his big winged chair with his feet on a footstool, fast asleep. His snores followed them as they went down the steps and into the blaze of the afternoon sun.

"Golly, I don't think I've ever been anywhere so hot," said Harriet. "I can't believe people can work outdoors in this heat."

They headed across the road and down the path to an old wooden jetty jutting out into the water. The edge of the lake was weedy and there was no beach, so the best way into the water was off the end of the jetty, which had a ladder attached to make getting out easier.

"Last one in is a cowardly custard," yelled Molly as she slipped off her sandshoes and took a running jump into the water.

Sophie was about to suggest that they check the depth before jumping in, but before she could come out with this prudent course of action, there were four more splashes. She quickly joined the others. The relief of cooling off was delicious. The lake was plenty deep enough for diving, and soon they were all practising their dives and racing out to a floating log and back. The water was a lot warmer than the ocean in Vancouver had been, but it was still refreshing. They alternated between drying off on the jetty and jumping in again to cool off.

"I don't think we should lie in the sun too much," said Sophie. "We don't want anyone to get sunburn and have to stay behind when we go on the cattle drive."

Sophie, Molly, Mark, and Posy spent the rest of the day until dinner lazing under the willow trees with books. Harriet joined them but opted to update her journal with all the events of the day. Leticia prowled round the hotel and barn taking photographs. She had four rolls of film with her, with twelve exposures on each roll, so she had to ration the number of pictures she took. She chose the subject and composed her photographs carefully before releasing the shutter. She took one of the front of the hotel, one of the barn with several horses tied up outside, and one of the children lounging under the trees with the lake in the background.

After a delicious dinner of roast chicken followed by home-bottled cherries and ice cream, the children went upstairs. It was still dusk, and they had no need to light their oil lamps. Before night had fully fallen they were all fast asleep.

THE NEXT MORNING everyone except Posy was feeling the effects of their first day in the saddle. Captain Gunn could hardly walk, and the walking he did was a bow-legged stagger. However, they were all determined to persevere, and everyone except Captain Gunn soon had their "horse legs."

The next few days followed a similar schedule: riding lessons in the morning followed by swimming and exploring the area around the hotel and barn in the afternoon. They learned that the ranch attached to the hotel was close to 28,000 acres and that they ran 1,500 head of cattle.

By the third day everyone except Captain Gunn was doing very well with their riding and could now walk, trot, and canter.

Captain Gunn struggled, but his horse, Rocky, was extremely patient and bore the large bulk of his passenger bouncing up and down in the saddle with fortitude.

After the second day Posy graduated from the lessons and spent each morning riding out with her new cowboy friends, Gerry and Joey. At first Joey had been reluctant to have a small girl tagging along, but Posy soon proved herself to be a competent rider who took instructions well and was actually a real help. She was in seventh heaven, cantering over the range checking fences and gates and spotting groups of cattle and their calves. If she could have frozen herself in time she would have done. Posy could hardly bear to imagine leaving Spotty and the ranch behind, but being a sensible little girl she decided to enjoy every moment and not worry too much about partings, which were still some time ahead.

On the fourth day, after their riding lessons and lunch, the children headed down to the lake as usual. This time, however, there was a surprise waiting for them. Two small wooden sailing dinghies, each with a set of oars and a sail wrapped around a mast, were tied to the jetty.

Molly gave a whoop.

"I just knew Uncle Bert had a surprise up his sleeve!" she said. "He's been acting as if he couldn't wait to tell us something. I saw him and Mr. Schwimmer talking yesterday and they shut up when they saw me coming."

Captain Gunn joined them on the jetty.

"You've been doing really well with your riding lessons, and Sam says that you are almost ready to ride with him and the other cowboys on the cattle drive. Me, well that's a different matter, but I'm working on it. I've absolutely no intention of sitting in the wagon while the rest of you ride the range! Anyway, I've rented these dinghies for you for a couple of days and I thought you could go for an overnight camp-out across the lake. Apparently there's a lovely spot just across from us here with a nice beach and good place to camp. Mr. Schwimmer is arranging for some camping gear for us for the cattle drive, so you will have bedrolls ready to go. No need for tents in this climate. Also, Rose is going to pack you some food and cooking gear. I suggest you play around in them this afternoon, and tomorrow after riding you can go for the rest of the day and camp overnight. You'd better be back for your riding lessons the next day. Sam told me that the cattle drive will begin at 6:00 a.m. sharp on Friday, three days from now, and in any case I'm sure Posy won't want to miss a day of riding!"

They agreed to leave early enough the day after their camp-out to get back to the ranch in time for breakfast and riding.

Captain Gunn headed back to the hotel, and the others divided themselves between the two dinghies, rigged the masts and sails, and were soon rowing out into the lake hoping to catch a breeze.

There was very little wind, and what there was came in puffs every few minutes. Nobody minded because it was wonderful to be out on the water again. They sailed a bit, drifted a bit, and rowed a bit before tying the dinghies back at the jetty, tidying up, and walking back to the hotel.

THE NEXT DAY, after a shortened riding lesson, the children met Rose in the kitchen.

"I've got some of our homemade sausages here. I wrapped them up and put them in a bag with ice, so they should stay cool, but as soon as you get to the campsite you should sink them at the edge of the lake with some stones on top. Don't want anyone coming down with food poisoning before the cattle drive! Here's a couple of cans of beans and a nice hunk of my fresh sourdough bread. And here is a treat for dessert."

She brought out a small basket lined with a napkin with some fresh raspberries nestled inside.

"Put this basket somewhere it won't get squashed," she instructed. "Here's Sam now with your camping gear."

Sam had appeared at the back door with Joey. Between them they carried six bedrolls.

"You'll be taking these on the cattle drive. The cowboys' bedrolls are usually just a couple of blankets, but we keep these for guests who might appreciate a bit more comfort. You'll find a sleeping bag rolled up between two blankets. Make sure you put one of the blankets underneath the sleeping bag." Sam said. "Good practice having a night out with them before we leave. No need of tents here; it hardly ever rains in the summertime. Now if you're not as tough as Joey you can cut a bunch of pine branches to put underneath your beds and then settle yourselves around the campfire for the night. One thing you need to be very careful about is bears."

Here Mark's ears perked up. On their last trip they had seen many marine mammals and heard the howling of wolves, but they hadn't seen any bears, and he had gone back to England disappointed. It sounded like he might have more luck here.

"When you've had your dinner," continued Sam, "use one of the ropes off your boat to haul the bag with any leftover food up high between two trees. Bears have a great sense of smell, but they won't be able to reach your bag if you string it high enough."

Posy, Harriet, and Leticia exchanged looks of alarm.

Soon the whole gang were down at the dock loading the dinghies with the bedrolls, a fry pan, tin dishes, and food. Sophie added a small bag with soap and tooth powder (she was the only one to think of that), and before long they had cast off and were heading out into the lake.

The wind situation was similar to the day before, but as they reached the middle of the lake they spotted a dark patch on the water fast approaching from the north end. It sped across the flat water towards them, and suddenly the sails filled. Now they were sailing! The dinghies heeled over, everyone shifted to the upwind side, and the boats skimmed across the water towards the other side of the lake.

"Gosh, that was a great sail," said Molly, as they dowsed the sails and grounded on the gravel beach. "Almost as good as on the loch at home."

They scouted the area around the beach and found a perfect campsite a few yards from the water. It looked as if people had camped there before, judging from the ring of stones forming a firepit and the lack of overhanging branches to catch fire.

Everyone gathered firewood and got a great campfire going. Just to see what it would look like, they unrolled their bedrolls around the fire and Leticia took a photograph of everyone posing on their beds. They figured they weren't as tough as the cowboys and decided to gather some fragrant pine branches to pad their beds. Everything was put to one side for bedtime, and they spent the next couple of hours playing in the lake.

Finally Sophie declared that it was nearly suppertime, so they stoked up the fire and Sophie set the fry pan on a trio of flat stones. The sausages sizzled nicely, and they opened the cans of beans and set the whole cans in the embers to heat up.

They tucked into their camp supper of sausages, beans, and great hunks of bread and butter. Bottles of cola had been kept cool in the lake along with the sausages, and after finishing up with the raspberries, they declared that it was the best campfire dinner they had ever had. The location in the British Columbia wilderness with the possibility of bears lurking in the forest added an extra element of adventure.

They rinsed off their plates in the lake, scrubbed the fry pan with fine gravel, and set up the beds around the fire. What remained of the food was put into a canvas bag and slung up on a line between two trees, about fifty yards from the campsite. After washing their faces and hands and brushing their teeth, they all settled down facing inwards in a circle around the fire.

"I wonder what Ian's doing right now," mused Sophie.

"Probably learning how to properly swab the deck or doing drill exercises," laughed Molly. "I'll bet he's sorry he's missing all this." She made a grand sweeping gesture to the surrounding forest.

"I wish he was here right now," said Mark. "At least then I wouldn't be the only boy!"

"Oh, come now," said Sophie, tousling his hair. "Admit it. You like being surrounded by girls. We spoil you rotten!"

"Yeah, like when you left me at the train platform in Hope!"

Everyone laughed at the memory of Mark running after the train, but Sophie still felt guilty for nearly leaving him behind. What would the Girl Guides think!

"I know one thing," declared Molly. "If Ian was here right now he'd be telling one of his spectacular ghost stories!"

"Thank goodness he's not here, in that case!" said Posy in a quavering voice. "Those stories give me nightmares for weeks!"

"Really..." said Molly in a sly voice, pulling out a sheet of paper from the pocket of her shirt. "Well, I suppose you won't want to hear this little yarn Ian sent me just before we left on our trip. He said it's an authentic Canadian ghost story that takes place in the Interior of British Columbia on a hot summer night... Hmmm..." She paused for a moment, reading from the paper. "Well, isn't this a coincidence! The main characters are a group of six English children camping out on their own in the forest by a lake."

Posy covered her ears and buried her face in her bedroll, whimpering.

"For heaven's sake, Molly. Now look what you've done!" scolded Sophie. "Posy, don't worry. No one's going to tell that story. And I promise it's all made up anyway."

Molly ignored her and began to read from the paper in the same slow, eerie voice that Ian always used when telling ghost stories: "*It was a hot and muggy night, the sort of night that lures young children outdoors and drives the spirits into a violent frenzy...*"

"Molly!" yelled Sophie.

"What?" asked Molly innocently. "The story came from *your* brother, the impeccable student and soon-to-be naval hero."

"Yes, and you know as well as I that my brother can also be an expert tormentor of young children. Need I remind you how terrified you were the first time you heard one of his stories?"

"I was never terrified!"

"You were so! I was sleeping in the same room with you that night, remember? You kept the candle burning all night because you were so scared of the dark. You almost set the curtains on fire!"

"Oh, please," scoffed Molly, as if that was the most preposterous thing she'd ever heard. "I wasn't scared. I kept that candle burning because... because..."

"Because?" prompted Sophie.

"Because I was conjuring spirits," said Molly with a totally straight face.

Sophie looked at her and shook her head the way that her mother did when one of the children did or said something impossibly silly. On the surface there was disapproval, but there was always the hint of a smile, too. Molly could be so infuriating sometimes—well, a lot of the time, actually. But Sophie had to admit they'd had a lot of fun together.

She wasn't sure if she and Molly would ever have become friends if their families hadn't formed a bond first, but she was glad to have Molly around to stir up adventure and coax her out of her shell every now and then. However, she wasn't sure how Molly felt about having her around. Lately it seemed that every word Molly directed Sophie's way was laced with ridicule.

They bickered a bit more about the ghost story and whether it should be read out loud or not. Mark wanted to hear it; Harriet admitted she was intrigued but said she could read it to herself later… in the daylight. Leticia declared she was not a fan of the paranormal, and Posy had by now curled herself into a tiny ball and threatened to stay that way until people stopped saying the word "ghost." Finally Sophie changed the subject to the upcoming cattle drive and Posy's favourite subject—horses. The chatter went on far beyond their usual bedtime.

At last everyone started to drift off. The fire was down to glowing embers and the sky was a blanket of stars as they all dozed off to sleep.

A COUPLE OF hours later something woke Harriet. It was absolutely calm and still, and only a few remaining embers glimmered in the campfire. She found her torch and looked at her watch. It was 2 o'clock in the morning. What could have wakened her?

Then she heard it again. A definite rustling in the pine forest a short distance away.

She was wide awake by now and hissed at the others.

"Wake up, wake up, there's something strange going on!"

Everyone woke up and sat frozen in their bedrolls listening to the noises.

"I'll bet you that's a bear," whispered Leticia fearfully.

Molly took charge.

"Everyone go down to the lake and get the boats ready to launch if we have to escape in a hurry. Mark and I will go and take a look."

She looked around for her brother, and it was only then that the rest of the crew noticed that his sleeping bag was empty.

"Oh, no! The bear must have got him," said Leticia her teeth chattering.

"Don't be silly. He'll be fine. Let's go and look for him, over there where the noise is coming from."

Very quietly, holding their unlit torches, they crept away from the campsite and closer to the noise. As they approached the noise, it became clear what was causing it. Mark had loosened the rope that held the food cache in the tree and it had dropped into a bush. He was busy "raiding the larder" for a midnight snack.

"Shhh . . ." whispered Molly. "What a cheek. I'm going to give him the scare of his life."

Molly leapt out of the undergrowth with a piercing shriek, which caused Mark to drop his snack and fall backwards.

"You idiot!" he shouted. "You nearly gave me a heart attack!"

Everyone laughed because he sounded exactly like Captain Gunn.

The bag was raised once again into the tree and the children headed back to the campsite. They had barely settled down once more when they heard another noise coming from the direction of the food cache. This time the rustling was even louder and accompanied by a low grunting.

"That's a bear for sure," whispered Leticia.

"Well, I'm going back to take a look," said Molly.

There was no more talk of part of the crew waiting by the lake ready to evacuate—nobody wanted to be left behind—so the entire crew moved quietly back towards the food cache.

As they crouched behind a rock and their eyes got used to the dark, they could see what was going on. The food bag was hanging about fifteen feet off the ground, and in the faint light of the stars they could see a large creature standing on its hind legs and swiping with its front legs at the bag, which was clearly out of reach.

"Wow," whispered Mark, exhilarated. "*Finally* I see a bear. No one will believe this back at school. Too bad Leticia can't take a photograph to prove we saw it."

"Not sure letting off a flash would be the best thing to do right now," whispered Molly back.

They backed off and returned to the campsite, ready to head for the safety of the dinghies and the lake should they need to make their escape from a marauding bear. Leticia was shivering and Sophie was all for launching the boats until they were sure the bear had gone. After a few minutes, however, they heard the sound of the bear ambling away, obviously having given up on the food bag in the tree. Mark and Molly stole back to make sure he was gone, and once the all clear had been given everyone settled back into their bedrolls for the rest of the night. It had been another exciting chapter in their Canadian adventure!

CHAPTER FOUR

LEAVING THE QUILCHENA, FOR NOW

All the children woke up early after sleeping outside under the stars. Sophie said that any washing could wait until after their riding lesson, so they quickly packed up the dinghies and headed back across the lake.

Back at the hotel, they returned the cooking gear to Rose in the kitchen and stowed their bedrolls on the back porch. They would be needing them again soon.

After a quick breakfast they went to the barn, where Captain Gunn was already saddling up Rocky. The others quickly got their horses ready to join him in the big corral. Posy, as usual, was preparing to ride out on the range with her two cowboy friends.

Things seemed to be much busier than usual around the barns and corrals. Preparations for the cattle drive were gearing up. Cowboys came and went with saddles and bedrolls, and they noticed one man carrying a banjo. Why on earth would anyone need a banjo on a cattle drive?

Suddenly Molly stiffened and dug Captain Gunn in the ribs.

"Look," she hissed, "that's the cowboy we saw on the train, the one I thought looked familiar. I remember now where I've seen him! I'm almost certain he was one of our gang of villains that were trying to get their hands on Brother XII's treasure. I'm pretty sure he's not the one that shot me, but I remember him because he was the only one with fair hair, and I got a pretty good look at him when they were stuck on the rocks in Hole in the Wall."

Captain Gunn slowly turned and glanced sneakily at the young cowboy who was just about to disappear into the barn.

"You could be right," he said cautiously, "but I don't think we can be certain."

"But Uncle Bert. I swear he looks *exactly* like—"

"Now, now. Don't get excited. It might be him, and it might not. Better just keep an eye on him for now. We wouldn't want to go and tell Sam and possibly get him fired, would we?"

Molly looked doubtful.

"Plus, if it *is* him, and he's done his time in jail, I think he deserves a second chance, don't you?"

"Maybe," said Molly. "But I've got my eye on him, and I'm going to tell the others to watch him for any suspicious behaviour. You know what they say—a leopard never changes its spots."

"Sometimes that's true," Captain Gunn admitted. "But sometimes the leopard sheds its old spots and sprouts new, more...er...honest spots."

Molly raised an eyebrow.

"What I mean to say is, it looks like he's doing an honest day's work here, and I know the ringleader of that gang that shot you is still in jail, so this cowboy here—*if* he was part of that crew— is probably trying to turn his life around. And we shouldn't stand in the way of that. So, keep an eye on him, yes. Be careful around him? Absolutely. But don't go accusing him of anything or exposing his supposed past in front of everyone. Do I make myself clear?"

"All right," sighed Molly. "I suppose you're right."

Sam had been talking to a group of cowboys near the barn and came over to join the group. The other children had mounted their horses while Molly and Captain Gunn were talking.

"We ride out at dawn tomorrow," he began. "You all need to be down at the barn saddling up at half past five. Anyone not ready when we pull out will be left behind. Let's have a quick lesson today and then you will need to get your kit organized for the drive. Put your bags out on the back porch tonight and they will be loaded onto the wagon with all the other gear."

It was a bit like passing a test at school. Sam put them through their paces and declared them all ready to join the cattle drive. He was still slightly doubtful about Captain Gunn, but decided to keep his reservations to himself and just leave the option open for him to ride on the wagon. After all, it was Captain Gunn who was paying the bill.

"We're going to have a meeting this evening around five," continued Sam. "We'll all meet under the willows beside the hotel. You'll meet the whole crew, and we'll go over the rules, safety precautions, and what everyone's jobs are. We want to make sure that you don't get trampled by a herd of stampeding cattle, so you all need to pay attention."

AFTER LUNCH AND a swim—during which Molly filled the others in about her suspicions of the fair-haired cowboy—the children returned to the hotel to organize their gear for the trip. Sam had warned them to pack light, and Sophie quickly realized that she was going to have to let go of her usual standards of cleanliness. She would pack her first-aid kit, along with her small bag of hygiene necessities, namely soap and tooth powder, but clothes had to be kept to a minimum.

"Right," she said. "We'll have to reduce our luggage to a total of two bags, one for us Phillips children and one for the MacTavishes. Captain Gunn will have to organize his own gear. Everything not needed on the trip will be stored in the box room. I believe there are other guests staying in our rooms while we are away, but we'll get them back after the cattle drive."

They sorted out their clothes and decided to pack two clean shirts each, some clean underwear and socks, and a toothbrush and hairbrush each. Harriet added her notebook, and Leticia was not going to be parted from her precious camera. She couldn't wait to get some photographs of the cattle and cowboys in action, and it occurred to her that getting close enough to the cowboys, and the fair-haired one in particular, might be a good excuse to see if he got up to anything suspicious.

There was still some time before the meeting at five, so they decided that now would be a good time to write postcards home to their parents. They crossed the blazing hot area between the hotel and the store and dove into the cool of the old building. There was a rack of postcards by the cash register with sepia photos of old ranching scenes. There was a great one of the hotel, which Sophie decided she would send to her mother. The others chose one each and the lady behind the cash register was able to sell them stamps that would get the postcards all the way from Quilchena to England. As well they couldn't resist the sticks of coloured candy and bought one each with the pocket money their parents had given them before they left England. They'd exchanged their pounds into dollars in Vancouver, so they were not entirely dependent on Captain Gunn for treats.

Everyone took their stamped postcards over to the shady area under the willow trees.

"Dear Mummy and Daddy," wrote Posy. "I am having the best time of my life and can ride as well as the cowboys!"

Not quite true, but pretty close!

Molly wrote about the possible encounter with one of their old villains, Leticia wrote about documenting the expedition on film, Sophie wrote about the wonderful hotel and Canadian food, and Mark recounted their bear encounter in full detail. That left Harriet, who covered her postcard with small sketches copied out of her notebook.

AS FIVE O'CLOCK approached, cowboys started to trickle in around the side of the hotel carrying bottles of beer. Captain

Gunn grabbed a beer for himself (deciding to go cowboy style this evening instead of drinking his usual whisky) and told the children to fetch themselves a drink.

They ran round and into the bar where the barman served them ice-cold bottles of cola. At the beginning of their stay they had wondered how, in a hotel without electricity, it was possible to have ice cream and ice on hand. Rose had explained to them.

"It gets mighty cold here in the winter and the lake freezes over several feet deep. The crews go out with sleighs and cut big blocks of ice and then bring them back to put into the icehouse. You can see it out back behind the hotel. The icehouse is dug down like a pit and lined with straw. Then they pack the blocks of ice inside and pile straw over them, and there's a thick roof to top it all off. You wouldn't believe it in this heat, but that ice lasts through until it freezes again."

It was hard for the children to imagine the place in the depths of winter. But they had seen the photos from Captain Gunn's book research, and some of them showed horses pulling sleighs with bundled-up passengers. Some of the horses had icicles hanging off their noses, and the people looked like they would much rather be inside beside a roaring fire!

Soon everyone was sitting on the grass under the trees with their drinks, and Sam called the meeting to order.

"I always like to get everyone together before a cattle drive, and it's real important this time with our guests along. Everyone needs to know their place, and there are some important rules that we need to follow for everyone's safety. First let's do the introductions. Raise your hand when I call your name."

He called the children and Captain Gunn's names first and then moved on to the cowboys.

"You already know Gerry and Joey," he said as the two cowboys raised their bottles. "Over there are Thomas and Charlie. They're from the Douglas Lake Indian band and a finer pair of cowboys you won't find west of the Rocky Mountains!"

The children had seen the two Native cowboys around the barn, but they were shy and had hardly spoken.

"Over there is our rookie cowboy, Norm, who arrived the same day you did."

Molly stiffened and turned to look the fair-haired young cowboy dead in the eye, but he avoided looking directly at her or the others. If she wasn't sure before, Molly was now certain that this was the young man she had last seen scrambling up the rocks away from the wreck of the *Black Pearl* in the treacherous waters of Hole in the Wall. If he thought he could avoid her forever, he was very much mistaken.

"And to round out the crew, we have our two mud pups—that's what we call Englishmen who come out to try their hand at ranching. Robert and George, say hello to your fellow countrymen!"

Robert and George stood up and shook the hands of each the children in turn. They spoke with accents that would have been more at home in Oxford than in the wilds of British Columbia. They explained that they had just arrived back at the ranch after a week off in Vancouver, which was why the children had not seen them before.

"And last, but definitely not least, we have Wee Tan, our talented cook. Be nice to him, or you won't get anything to eat!"

A Chinese man with a long pigtail got up and bowed to everyone.

"Now this is a bit of an unusual cattle drive. Normally we'd be driving cattle from one grazing area to another, or we'd be driving them to the train at Nicola, sending them on their way to market in Vancouver. However, we've had a request for 250 head of cattle to be delivered to Fintry on Okanagan Lake. We're supplying one hundred and we are picking up another 150 at the Douglas Lake Ranch. It's about forty miles as the crow flies from here to Fintry. A dealer in Kelowna has bought them, and once we get them to Fintry they'll be loaded onto a barge and shipped down the lake. We reckon we can drive them about ten miles a day, so allowing for delays and rounding up strays, it should take us five days or so.

"The first day will be the longest—it's about sixteen miles from here to the Douglas Lake Ranch, but it's easy going, all along the road, so we should make it by dinnertime no problem."

Here Captain Gunn looked a bit worried. It was one thing to bounce around in the corral for a couple of hours each day, but five days straight in the saddle might just finish him off. The baggage wagon suddenly didn't seem such a bad idea.

"Right," said Sam, "we muster at first light tomorrow. Our one hundred head are in one of the outer corrals—the boys have brought them in over the past few days, with the expert help of young Posy here!"

Posy blushed and looked modest, but she knew her riding skills had taken a giant leap forward over the past week, and she had been keeping up with the other cowboys and become handy at turning stray cattle back to the herd. She and Spotty had developed into an efficient team.

"So—be ready to ride out at 6:00 a.m. tomorrow. You lot," and here he pointed to the children and Captain Gunn, "are to ride well behind the herd, with Gerry to keep you company. He'll get you out of trouble if necessary. Posy, you can ride along with Joey and do what he says. We should be at the Douglas Lake Ranch by late afternoon. They're laying on dinner and bunkhouses for the crew, and we'll be staying there two nights to get the cattle sorted and ready to move both herds out the next day. Any questions?"

No one had any, so the meeting broke up. Sam took the children and Captain Gunn aside.

"Mr. Ward, the manager over at the Douglas Lake Ranch, has invited all of you to dinner with him in the big house tomorrow evening. Mr. Cameron, you'll stay in the house, and you kids have been assigned your own bunkhouse."

The children and Captain Gunn chatted for a while with the cowboys, except Norm, who, with a glance over his shoulder, slunk off behind the hotel. Molly casually got up and followed him round the back and over to the barn area. She got close enough to Norm to make him jump and take off at speed towards the cowboys' bunkhouses, which were out of bounds to paying guests. She rushed back to the others to tell them what had happened. If Norm's skittish behaviour wasn't enough to convince everyone that he was bad news, she didn't know what was.

"I'll admit, he does seem like a very nervous sort of chap," said Leticia, "but maybe he's just afraid of girls."

"Especially brazen girls who chase him behind a barn!" said Sophie. "Honestly, Molly! What if he's just shy? You're not exactly the demure sort. You probably scared him to death!"

"Whose side are you two on, anyway?" asked Molly indignantly. "Yesterday when I told you about him you were as suspicious as I was. And today when he refused to make eye contact with anyone during the meeting—that was strange, wasn't it? And if he had nothing to hide, why wouldn't he stick around and chat when I followed him? Shy boys don't join pirate gangs that shoot girls on boats in cold blood!"

Sophie, Leticia, Harriet, and Mark looked at each other. Dramatic though she was, they all had to admit Molly had a point.

But there was no time to discuss the matter any further. Tonight everyone (including the cowboys) had to be in bed long before night fell. They would have an early start the next day.

IT SEEMED AS if they had hardly gone to sleep when a tapping on their doors awakened them. It was Rose, who had been up since 4 o'clock helping Wee Tan with the final packing of the baggage and food wagon.

"I've got some coffee and fresh bread ready for you downstairs," she whispered, not wanting to wake the other guests who were unlucky enough to not be going on a cattle drive.

Washing was a minimal affair, and then the bags that were to be left behind were put out in the hallway, before the gang tiptoed downstairs to the dining room.

Captain Gunn was already gulping down a large mug of coffee and had a huge slab of bread spread with a thick layer of home-churned butter and Rose's famous preserves. Clearly he didn't want to start the cattle drive without a full stomach.

The children joined him, and Rose brought them mugs of their own with lots of cream and sugar so they could drink up without scalding their tongues.

"I've got a water bottle each for you by the back door, and a snack to see you through until lunchtime," she said.

"How are we going to carry them on our horses?" said Leticia. "Also, I forgot to ask, but I want to have my camera handy, and not packed with the other stuff in the wagon."

"Don't worry," replied Rose. "Sam has found small saddlebags for you all, and you'll have room for personal items as well as your water bottles."

"Good," said Sophie. "I'm going to keep my first-aid kit handy."

"And I'm going to put my diary and pencils in my bag," said Harriet. "That way if we stop for lunch I can jot down things I might forget if I don't write them down straight away."

It was now just before 5:30 a.m., so they all quickly finished their breakfasts and headed out to the barn.

Gerry, Joey, and the other cowboys were already tacking up and had been kind enough to bring the children's horses in from the corrals and tie them to the hitching rail. Norm was there, but he wasn't much help because he seemed afraid to come anywhere near the children or their horses. Instead, he hung around in the background pretending to look busy while not actually doing anything. Molly found this very suspicious indeed.

After a week of practice, everyone was pretty competent with the brushes and tack and got their horses ready in record time. Joey helped them attach their saddlebags, which lay across the back of the horse, just behind the saddle, tied on with leather laces.

Everyone mounted (or in Captain Gunn's case, heaved himself clumsily onto the long-suffering Rocky) and the whole crew of cowboys and guests stood ready for the off.

Wee Tan and his wagon, pulled by the same pair of horses that had fetched them from the station, drove over from the cookhouse where the last few items had been loaded. The wagon now had been fitted with a hooped canvas cover, presumably to keep everything dry if it should rain and provide some protection from the sun. Everyone waited for Sam to give the signal.

"Robert and George have gone ahead to open the gates," said Sam, who was mounted on his horse, Rover, a huge bay with four white socks and a full white face. They knew that Rover was a cross between a thoroughbred and a Clydesdale and looked every bit the boss of all the other horses. He was the perfect mount for Sam, chief wrangler and cow boss.

"The first part of the drive is easy," he said. "It's along the road between here and Douglas Lake. Once we turn off the main road, there are fences on both sides, so the cattle will naturally follow the road. We don't have any yahoo cowboys on this ranch—we like to keep the cattle moving ahead slow and steady. That way they won't be stressed and we are less likely to have a stampede."

The cattle had been corralled in a large fenced area a short distance from the barn. The children and Captain Gunn waited on the other side of the fence while the cowboys went in and quietly shepherded the cattle out of the gate and onto the road. As the last of the cattle streamed by, the children and Captain Gunn fell in behind with their chaperone, Gerry, riding beside them.

"Golly," said Molly, "we're actually driving cattle in the Wild West!"

It wasn't sailing, but it was an adventure none of them could have dreamed of back in their English boarding schools. Their friends were going to need Leticia's photographs to prove it had actually happened.

THE FIRST PART of the drive was along the main road that passed in front of the hotel. A couple of cowboys had ridden ahead to block the road and make sure that the cattle all turned right onto the road that led to the Douglas Lake Ranch. Once they had made the turn, the road narrowed and took a meandering route, following a creek on the left, which they could occasionally see over the fence that edged the road. The cowboys strung themselves out along both sides of the herd, with Posy sticking close to Joey, but really there was nowhere for the cattle to go except forwards, and they obediently followed the road.

Soon, the drive settled down into a steady rhythm and they made good progress. The sun was climbing into the sky and already it felt hot. The children were glad of their water bottles and by 9 o'clock had already pulled out their snacks, eating them on the go.

Captain Gunn's face got redder and redder, and he mopped his bow with increasing frequency.

"Darned if I'm going to give up on the first day," he muttered to himself.

Finally Sam rode back from where he had positioned himself near the front of the herd and told everyone they were going to take a lunch stop.

"There's a gate just ahead on the left, and we'll drive the herd through and over to the creek so they can drink and graze for a bit. I can see Wee Tan not far behind; he'll pull the wagon into the shade of those trees on the other side of the fence. Everyone ride down to the creek and give your horses a drink and then tie them up to the trees and take a break."

No one, Captain Gunn least of all, was going to argue with that! Soon the cattle had been turned into their temporary pasture and were all standing knee deep in the creek having a nice cool drink. The horses were watered and then the children, Captain Gunn, and the cowboys all congregated under the trees. The horses were happy to doze in the shade with their girths loosened, while the humans enjoyed their lunch of cold beef sandwiches. The back of the wagon was fitted with a box containing cupboards and drawers, which were hidden behind a folding table that dropped down and provided a work top. Wee Tan had fired up a portable stove in his mobile kitchen and brewed coffee, drunk sweet and black by the cowboys. The children refilled their water bottles from the large barrel slung underneath the wagon.

After downing their lunches everyone lay down in the shade near the horses and had a nap. Molly tried to stay awake to keep an eye on Norm, and encouraged the other children to do so as well, but before long their fatigue got the better of them and they were all snoozing peacefully. It had been an early start, and the day was only half done.

Sooner than they would have wished, Sam gave the signal to mount their horses. Thomas and Charlie quietly circled the herd and pushed them through the gate and back onto the road.

The next few hours proved to be an endurance test for all the guest cowboys except Posy. There was no more chatting; they just endured the increasing agony of sitting on their horses. What Captain Gunn was feeling he kept to himself, but his face was beet red, and he hung onto the horn of his saddle with a look of increasing desperation. Sophie glanced at him and sincerely hoped he wasn't about to collapse.

Everyone scanned the road ahead for any sign of the Douglas Lake Ranch, and finally, as the heat of midday eased slightly as late afternoon approached, they saw the glint of water ahead.

"That must be Douglas Lake," gasped Molly, once again mopping her brow with her silk kerchief—which was turning out to be a lifesaving purchase indeed. When the dust kicked up by the cattle ahead had been especially thick, the children found that pulling their kerchiefs up over their mouths and noses stopped them from choking.

"I studied the map before we left the hotel," said Harriet, "and it's about another four miles to the actual ranch."

Seeing the lake breathed new life into everyone, and even Captain Gunn perked up and looked like he was going to finish the day's ride still in the saddle.

The cattle and cowboys crossed a bridge over the creek and turned right along the road that now edged the lake. They were not stampeding, but it was as if the cattle sensed that their day was almost over and they began to speed up. Soon everyone was moving at a jog, which inflicted further pain on the guest cowboys, but no one was going to call it quits at this stage in the game. The road followed the edge of the lake for a few more miles and then crossed another creek, took a sharp turn to the right, and passed between some cultivated fields. Not a moment too soon, the whole herd, the cowboys, and Wee Tan with the wagon were passing through the ranch gates. They had survived the first day of the drive.

CHAPTER FIVE

THE DOUGLAS LAKE RANCH

T he entrance to the ranch was a massive post-and-beam gateway, with a carved and painted sign hanging from the crosspiece. The cattle and the cowboys streamed in under the sign, and the cowboys on the flank of the herd turned the cows off to the left. Sam rode back towards the children and Captain Gunn.

"You've done a great job, but the pros will take it from here," he said with a chuckle.

This was huge relief to everyone, but most of all to Captain Gunn, who looked as if he was about to slide off his horse into the dust.

"Mr. Ward is expecting you," Sam continued. "Ah, here he comes with the welcoming committee."

The cattle had churned up a huge cloud of dust that had obscured what lay beyond the gate. As it settled, three figures emerged, two men and a woman. They approached the group of amateur cowboys, who were still mounted. Everyone except Posy was slouched in their saddles wearing pained expressions.

One of the figures spoke. "Hello there. I'm Frank Ward. Welcome to the Douglas Lake Ranch. You look like you've all had just about enough for the day, so get yourselves off those horses."

He waved a hand, and a couple of young cowboys came hurrying over. The children managed more or less graceful dismounts, but Captain Gunn had to be helped off his horse and stood shakily with the children in front of the reception committee.

Frank Ward did not look like the manager of a ranch the size of an English county. He would have looked more at home behind the counter of a hardware store. He was of medium build and wore a crumpled linen suit and tie with a battered felt hat to top off his outfit. He appeared to be in his mid- to late sixties, and they later learned that he had just decided to retire, having run the ranch for almost thirty years.

The young cowboys led the horses away, and Frank turned to the man standing beside him.

"This is Joe Coutlee, my cow boss, and you won't find a better cow boss this side of the Rockies."

Over six feet tall, Joe towered over Frank. He looked like he could stop a runaway truck with one hand. His height was exaggerated by his tall ten-gallon hat, and he wore a massive pair of fringed chaps. The children felt like midgets beside him, but as he gazed over the group his face lit up with a giant smile.

"You folk look just about all done in," he said.

"That's the understatement of the century," muttered Molly, rubbing the inside of her knees. "I don't think I'll be able to walk upright for days."

The third member of the welcoming committee stepped forward.

"Hello there. I'm Kenny Ward. We'll soon have you sorted out and feeling better."

Kenny was surprisingly elegant for a ranch wife. Rather than the jeans and checked shirts the women at the Quilchena had worn, she was dressed in a full divided skirt that reached down to her calves, topped with a silk shirt. Her waist was cinched with a belt studded with silver, and she wore a beautiful silver and turquoise necklace. Her iron-grey hair was neatly cropped, and her hat was trimmed with a turquoise-studded leather band.

"Right," she said, taking charge. "Frank, you get Mr. Cameron over to the house, and I'll take you young folk to your cabin. Joe, can you make sure that Wee Tan sorts out the baggage and gets everyone's bags to the right place?"

The children looked around with interest. The ranch looked like a good-sized village, with dozens of buildings ranging from tiny cabins to several large barns. There was even a small church. All the buildings were painted white and roofed in red. White fences lined the lanes, and they could see corrals, cattle chutes, an open blacksmith shed, tractors, and other machinery neatly lined up. Everywhere men were going about the business of working a massive ranching operation. Joe strode off to the baggage wagon, and Wee Tan parked outside one of the larger buildings.

Kenny led them down a laneway away from the main group of buildings. She stopped outside a neat cabin with a porch and hitching rail outside.

"This is it. I think you'll be comfortable here."

They followed her up the steps, over the porch and into the cabin. Inside it was neat, clean, and very spartan. There were four tiers of bunks lining the walls, chairs set around a table, hooks on the walls, and a pot-bellied stove against one wall. A second door let out the back, and Kenny beckoned them to follow. Outside, shielded by trees and bushes, was a shower. Beside it was a single tap over an old porcelain sink.

"The water comes from a tank on the roof, so it'll be nice and warm. I'm sure you will feel like cleaning up, so why don't you all shower and change, and I'll send a cowboy over in an hour to show you the way to the house. Dinner is at 6:30."

And with that she left them, walking briskly back the way they'd come.

"Phew," said Harriet. "I could fall down and sleep on the floor!"

"We'll all feel better after we've showered," said Sophie. "But why don't we choose our bunks and rest while we take turns in the shower."

There was a knock at the open front door, and Wee Tan poked his head inside.

"Got all your stuff here," he said.

Two cowboys accompanied him, lugging their bags and bedrolls. They dumped everything just inside the door and disappeared.

Everyone picked a bunk, unrolled their bedrolls on top of the straw mattresses, and dug out clean clothes. There was a bit of disagreement as to who should get to shower first, as they were all desperate to wash off the dust. They agreed to go in order of age, which made Posy last, but as she was the one who had fared best and looked as if she could ride for another twenty miles, she didn't mind.

The crew lolled on their bunks until their turn for the shower, and in half an hour they were all washed, brushed, and dressed in clean, if somewhat wrinkled, clothes.

"We're going to be here for two days," said Sophie. "I'll ask Mrs. Ward if there's somewhere we can rinse out the jeans and shirts we wore today. We might as well start the next leg of the trip with clean clothes."

Molly was too tired to think of a proper dig at Sophie's obsession with cleanliness, so she just let it go. She was also too tired to go spying on Norm, which had been her original plan for that evening after dinner. There would be time for all that tomorrow after a decent night's sleep.

Just before 6:30 there was a knock on the door. It was Joe Coutlee, the cow boss. He had changed and was now dressed in spotless blue jeans and a smartly pressed shirt with a leather lace tie boasting a fabulous silver ornament. A pair of shiny, elaborately embossed boots completed his outfit.

"I'm joining you for dinner in the big house," he explained, "so I thought I'd show you the way over."

Everyone followed him as he led the way to the edge of the "village" and along a gravel road. A short distance away, set in its own grounds, was the ranch house. Instead of the red and white of the ranch buildings, the house was white with a green roof and trim. As they approached they saw a large front garden, bounded by a white picket fence and a row of poplar trees. The house itself was large, with a wide veranda running round two sides. The group went through the front gate and up the steps to the veranda, where Kenny Ward met them.

"Welcome," she said. "You'll find your uncle round the corner relaxing in the shade. I'm afraid today has been a bit much for him. Go and join him and I'll bring out some drinks."

Joe and the children joined Captain Gunn, who was lounging on a long wicker chair, with a drink on a small table beside him. He looked somewhat restored, having bathed and changed into his idea of dinner wear—an extremely crumpled pair of linen trousers held up by his new suspenders and a gaily patterned cotton shirt. His feet were bare.

"Ahoy there," he said from the depths of his chair. "Jolly fine place, this, and everything seems a lot better with a glass of good Scottish whisky!"

"Are you all right, Uncle Bert?" said Leticia. "We were afraid that you were going to collapse and we'd all have to miss the rest of the cattle drive."

"Thanks for your concern," laughed her uncle. "I do admit that today went far beyond what I had imagined a day in the saddle could be, but I'll be fine after a day of being pampered by the estimable Mrs. Ward."

Mrs. Ward appeared on cue through a set of French doors that led onto the veranda. She carried a tray with glasses full of ice and six bottles of cola.

"Sit down and relax," she said, putting the tray down on a wicker table. "Frank will be out in a minute, and we can have a nice chat before dinner. We don't get many guests here and I'm looking forward to using my best china in the dining room, rather than eating in the kitchen as we usually do."

Frank joined them, and a half hour of pleasant conversation passed quickly, despite the fatigue they all felt. The Wards were fascinated by the story of their previous adventures on the coast, tracking down Brother xii's treasure.

"We read about it in the paper at the time," said Kenny, "but we never imagined we'd meet the intrepid crew who succeeded in finding the gold."

Talk turned to Captain Gunn's current project, the very reason for their presence at the Douglas Lake Ranch.

"As you know from our correspondence, we have a lot of records and photos that I think will be a great help in your research," said Frank to Captain Gunn. "Tomorrow we'll spend some time in the library going through storage boxes, and then I'll leave you to get on with it."

"What would you children like to do tomorrow?" asked Kenny.

Sophie mentioned the laundry issue, and Kenny offered to let her use the laundry room in the basement.

"We have a washer with a wringer, and the weather's so hot that even your blue jeans will be dry by the time you leave the following day."

The party moved inside for dinner. All the rooms had high ceilings and lots of beautiful old furniture. The dining room table looked big enough to seat twenty, and the meal served by Kenny with the assistance of Nellie, the maid, was delicious. They were becoming used to the large pieces of meat served at Canadian meals, and this dinner was no exception. The hungry crew ate steaks with nugget potatoes and fresh green peas, and finished off the meal with apple pie and thick cream.

"We grow most everything we eat," said Kenny, "and we eat very well!"

It was getting dark by the time the meal ended, and Kenny got up and lowered the chandelier that hung over the table, by means of a pulley and chain on the wall. She leaned over with a match and lit the five arms of the light fixture, which sprung into life with pops and fizzes. The room was immediately lit by light as bright as any electricity could provide.

"We have a calcium carbide plant which produces acetylene gas and gives us lovely bright light," explained Kenny. "It's great in the winter when we're shut in by snow and early evenings. We don't have to hunch over oil lamps to read or sew."

Talk turned to the interests of the children. Frank and Kenny were good listeners and were keen to know something of their guests' lives.

Leticia talked about her photography and what excellent subjects she was finding on their trip. Harriet was interested in gathering material for her future planned career as a writer/illustrator. Mark was very interested in the lighting system and was promised a tour before they left. Posy was, of course, thrilled by the horse culture she was experiencing.

"How about you, Molly?" asked Frank. "What do you like to do when you're not chasing pirate gold or riding the range?"

"I'm going to be a bush pilot when I grow up," said Molly. "I've been taking flying lessons in England and my instructor says I'll be ready to take the flight exams and get my licence as soon as I turn sixteen next year."

Frank was silent for a moment.

"We have an airstrip a mile or so from here, and I have a lovely little Gypsy Moth bi-plane. I use it for checking out the cattle on the range, and just for fun, too, I suppose. Kenny here isn't too keen on flying, so I'm always looking for willing passengers. How'd you like to go flying with me tomorrow?"

"Are you joking?!" shrieked Molly, jumping up out of her chair. "I'd love it!"

"Well, it's a date, then!" laughed Frank, delighted by this unexpectedly free-spirited young English girl.

"What about the rest of you?" asked Kenny.

"Well, except for doing the washing, I think we'd all like to just take it easy—maybe go for a swim in the lake, if that's all right," said Sophie, as calm and polite as Molly was loud and exuberant.

"How about you get the real cowboy experience and have breakfast with the boys in the cookhouse," said Kenny. "Nellie can pack you a picnic lunch and you can spend the afternoon by the lake. And of course you are all invited back here for dinner tomorrow night. Apart from anything else I'd love to hear how Molly enjoys her flight."

THE NEXT AFTERNOON, the small plane gathered speed and bounced along the rough landing strip before taking off like the moth it was named after.

Molly, seated in the right-hand seat beside Frank, gazed below her in rapture as the ground fell away. Flying was the best thing she had ever done; it was even better than her first love of sailing. There was such an incredible feeling of lightness and freedom as the wheels left the ground, with no dependence on the wind to fill the sails and no road to follow.

She had left the others after a breakfast of bacon and pancakes cooked by Wee Tan in the cookhouse. It had been fun gossiping with their cowboy friends from the Quilchena, and meeting new ones from the Douglas Lake Ranch.

"Didn't know they let girls fly," said Joey, grinning at Molly.

"Don't see why not," said Charlie, whose sister was the same age as Molly but a lot less adventurous. He'd been in awe of Molly's boldness since the moment he first saw her.

"Of course they do," said Molly. "Haven't you ever heard of Amelia Earhart?"

"Amelia who? Is that the name of your pretty friend over there?" asked Joey, nodding towards Sophie, who immediately turned a bright shade of pink.

"Oh, no," joked Molly with a dismissive wave of her hand. "Sophie wouldn't know how to fly a plane unless it doubled as a washing machine."

All the cowboys roared with laughter, and Sophie went from blushing pink to deep angry red. Molly caught a glimpse of her expression and instantly knew she'd gone too far. Although it was true that, after flying and sailing, teasing Sophie was one of Molly's favourite hobbies, like flying and sailing it was an activity that did not come without risk. She vowed to make it up to Sophie later.

Meanwhile, Norm was still keeping a low profile and had seated himself as far away from the children as possible. Did he really think they hadn't recognised him, thought Molly? She managed to catch his eye and give him one of her scariest glares, at which he went pale and practically buried his head in his plate of pancakes.

Joe Coutlee sat at the head of one of the two long trestle tables, and was obviously held in high esteem by the rest of the men.

The children dispersed after breakfast. Mark, Leticia, Harriet, Sophie, and Posy headed for the ranch house with their Laundry. Frank picked up Molly outside their bunkhouse in a beat-up old pickup truck.

"I've left your uncle with a stack of old books and photographs, and he's in his element. He was scribbling like crazy when I left. I think he's going to have a great book when all's said and done," Frank chuckled. "Not sure how keen he is on getting back on Rocky tomorrow, but he seems pretty tough."

Frank, with Molly riding shotgun, bounced along a rough road until they reached the airstrip. Together they pushed the little plane out of its hangar. Molly helped Frank do all the pre-flight checks that she had learned from her instructor, and they climbed aboard, strapped themselves in, and took off.

Now Frank circled the plane over the ranch buildings. They looked like toys set in a model farmyard. Molly spotted the ranch house and waved madly at Kenny and the rest of the crew standing on the lawn.

"How about you take the controls?" said Frank through his headphones. "Your uncle says you are doing very well with your lessons, so let's see how you handle a strange plane."

The plane had dual controls, so Molly grasped the control column, took a deep breath, and said, "I have control," as she had been taught to do.

"We'll head over towards Okanagan Lake," said Frank, pointing slightly to the right of where they were flying. "It's pretty well due east of where we are, so keep an eye on your compass. It's about thirty miles as the crow flies, and we're up here with the crows!"

Their flight path quickly took them away from any signs of civilization. The terrain was hilly, with great open spaces of golden grassland interspersed with stands of trees. They could see faint tracks crisscrossing the land and the odd small lake or pond fringed with bright green. Occasionally they spotted groups of cattle contentedly grazing the range.

"Keep her steady at two thousand feet above ground," said Frank.

Molly was concentrating on her flying in a way that would really have impressed her school teachers if she had been applying herself in the same way to her lessons in history and geography! Her gaze switched from looking out of the window, scanning the horizon for other planes (there weren't any— apart from the birds they were quite alone), to checking her instruments.

After about twenty minutes, Frank pointed out the front window.

"Look, there's the lake."

The hills fell away behind them and suddenly they were over water. The huge lake stretched in both directions, and they were heading across it towards hills on the opposite side.

"How about you try a landing?" suggested Frank. "Just do some big circles and we'll talk it through. There's an airport in Vernon across the lake and slightly to the north."

Molly went through a mental checklist of the landing procedures she had been taught. Flaps, throttle, check airspeed.

Frank knew where they were going and didn't add navigation to Molly's tasks.

"Know what you're doing?" he asked. "We're about five miles from the airport, so get yourself set up. Gradual descent to eight hundred feet and I'll talk you through it. I'll point the way."

They did a couple of circles before straightening out and crossing the lake, turning slightly to the north and descending over the outskirts of a small town.

"There it is," said Frank. "Get yourself lined up for your final approach. Flaps ten degrees, throttle back to sixty knots."

The small plane approached the runway, now clearly visible to Molly. The little Moth floated over the threshold, as the young pilot lifted the nose slightly and pulled back on the throttle so that the plane landed lightly on the runway.

"Well done, Molly. That was a perfect landing! I couldn't have done better myself!"

Molly grinned in delight as she taxied the plane over to the small airport building and came to a halt. She unclasped her hands from the control column and relaxed in her seat.

"Don't forget your shut down checklist," said Frank. "We'll go and have a nice cold drink before you fly us back."

FRANK DROPPED MOLLY off back at the cabin. The others were all sitting on the porch and jumped up when Molly arrived.

"That was unbelievable," said Molly, flopping down on the top step. "Frank let me land in Vernon and take off again and I practically flew the whole way there and back. I had a good view of where we are going on the cattle drive. It's going to take a lot longer on horseback than it did in a plane. Can you believe it only took twenty minutes to fly from her to the lake?" She looked around at her sister and friends. "What did you get up to all day?"

"Oh, you know, the usual," grinned Leticia. "Doing your laundry and generally being the support team for our very own soon-to-be-famous pilot!"

Sophie gave Molly a look but said nothing. She was clearly still cross from this morning, but she wasn't about to cause a scene about it.

The children headed back to the ranch house for dinner. Captain Gunn looked like he hadn't moved since the night before, lounging in the same chair with a glass of whisky.

"I've had the most splendid day," he said when the children arrived. He pointed to his notebooks that sat on the table along with a pile of reference books and old ledgers. Right on top of the pile was one labelled *Silver Mining in the Interior of British Columbia: A History from 1862 to 1923*. How was silver mining related to ranching, Harriet wondered.

"Those books are full of the most fascinating facts about this ranch as well as lots of information about ranching in general. I think my next book is going to be a huge hit back home. No one in England could imagine how big these places are and how many cattle they run. Do you know there are over thirteen thousand head of cattle out on the ranges belonging to this ranch? It's incredible! And there are lots of fascinating characters to put in the book. Joe Coutlee has quite a history and I'm hoping to get to know him over the next few days."

"How are you feeling about getting back on Rocky tomorrow?" asked Leticia.

"Actually, not too bad," replied her uncle. "Kenny has made a suggestion, and I think I will bow to the fact that I'm not as young and fit as I was and do what she says."

"And what's that?" asked Mark.

"Well, Kenny had a chat with Sam and Wee Tan, and they are going to set up a spot in the back of the wagon for me. I'll ride in the mornings and adjourn to the wagon after lunch. Rocky will follow behind."

Molly stopped herself from making fun of her uncle. She'd hurt enough feelings today with her teasing, and although she was pretty sure Captain Gunn could take it, sometimes it was impossible to tell what would offend people. So instead she put on her best Sophie voice and said, "That's a splendid idea. I was quite worried about you the other day."

THE NEXT MORNING, after an early breakfast in the cookhouse, the children and Captain Gunn once more found themselves mounted and ready for the off.

Posy was ecstatic to be reunited with Spotty, but the others viewed their mounts with various degrees of enthusiasm. Captain Gunn was less than delighted to be in the saddle again, but he had made his peace with the ever patient Rocky and was determined to ride at least the first part of the day without complaining.

Kenny had told them the night before that she intended to ride out with them for a couple of hours, and she now appeared from the direction of the house. Posy gasped. Kenny was mounted on the most beautiful horse she had ever seen, except for Spotty. The horse was snow white, with a rippling mane and tail, and Kenny was mounted side-saddle, sitting with an easy grace and looking like she had been born there.

As she approached the group she could see Posy's admiring glances.

"This is Gandalf," she said. "He's a purebred Andalusian and was a present from Frank last Christmas."

"That's a great name," said Posy, gazing in awe at the magnificent animal. "I've been reading *The Hobbit*, and I think a wizard's name is perfect for him."

"I hear you're a pretty good rider, Posy," said Kenny. "When you get back here after the cattle drive is over, how would you like to have a ride on him in the corral?"

Posy was completely speechless at such an invitation, and vowed to ride her very best while Kenny was along with them.

Sam and Joe, the two cow bosses, approached the group waiting for the signal to move on out. Sam was mounted on his huge bay, Rover, but Joe was riding a small chestnut horse.

"This is Jimbo," he said. "He might not look like much, but mark my words, this is one of the best cutting horses in the business."

"What's a cutting horse?" asked Posy.

"It means they can 'cut' a single cow out of a herd and get it separated so that we can work on it. Branding, dosing, vetting, whatever. They have competitions at the rodeos, and Jimbo here is the Western Canadian Cutting Champion."

Sam, Joe, and Kenny shepherded the visiting cowpokes along the road that led out of the village. Up ahead they could see the cattle milling around on the other side of a gate. The 150 head added from the Douglas Lake Ranch had swelled the herd, so they now had 250 cows to drive. It looked like an awful lot. Mark was wondering how they would sort them out at the other end, and asked Sam the question.

"Easy enough," Sam said. "They have different brands. The DLR used the three-bar brand, just three vertical lines, and the Quilchena uses a straight R brand. It's simple to sort and count the cattle. But in this case it's even simpler as we are selling the cattle as a herd of 250, and we know that we have contributed a hundred and the DLR has contributed 150. Even I can do the sums on that one!"

Wee Tan and his supply wagon joined them, and there had been some rearranging of cargo. Under the canopy, sitting amidships amongst all the trappings of a cattle drive on the move, sat a wicker chair. Captain Gunn was going to be quite comfortable on his afternoon respites in the wagon. Tied to the back of the wagon was a spare horse, equipped with a packsaddle. Joe explained that it was there in case some of the cowboys had to round up cattle that had wandered away from the drive and needed to be away from the main group overnight. The horse also served as a spare in case one of the other horses went lame.

Everyone was ready, with the Quilchena cowboys swelled by another four from the DLR. Sam was to ride on one side of the herd with his cowboys, and Joe was to ride the other side with his. As before, Gerry was assigned chaperone duties and fell in beside them, with Kenny at the other end of the group. She looked very impressive riding sidesaddle, as if it was just as easy as riding astride, which Posy knew was not the case. The whole crew, horses, professional cowboys, English cowpokes, and 250 head of cattle headed, out from the ranch on their journey across the range to Fintry. The cattle drive proper had started in earnest.

CHAPTER SIX
RIDING THE RANGE

The route followed a well-defined track, which wound away from the ranch and headed for the hills. The cattle spread out on either side of the track, but were contained by the cowboys riding the flanks. Wee Tan and his wagon brought up the rear. Molly couldn't help wondering what they would all look like from the air; having sped over the route the day before in the Gypsy Moth, she knew that by comparison they were moving at a snail's pace.

After an hour or so the riders at the rear of the herd stopped for a few minutes to let the cows and the dust get a bit farther ahead. Leticia pulled out her camera from her saddlebag and took a very artistic shot of the herd and its accompanying cloud of dust.

The trail wound upwards through open rangeland, with its rolling acres of bunch grass interspersed with clumps of pine trees. They were following the course of a small creek, which wound like a green ribbon through the predominately brown terrain. As the sun climbed up in the sky, it got hotter and hotter, and the English component of the cattle drive began to feel hot, dusty, and tired. All except Posy, who had ridden off with Kenny to round up a few cattle that had strayed too far from the main herd. She was again in seventh heaven, displaying her very best horse-riding skills to Kenny, who was extremely impressed by how well the little girl rode. There was no doubt that Posy would be getting a ride on Gandalf when they eventually returned to the ranch.

Not a moment too soon for Captain Gunn, Joe rode back to them and announced that they would be taking a lunch break. Wee Tan pulled his wagon into the shade of a stand of huge pine trees, and the weary cowpokes dismounted. The cattle strung themselves out along the small creek they had been following, standing and drinking before having their own lunch break, grazing on the plentiful bunch grass.

Everyone watered their horses and tied them in the shade, and Wee Tan produced lunch from his well-stocked wagon.

As the cowboys and children prepared to get going again, Kenny mounted Gandalf and turned him back the way they had come. Her splendid horse displayed his high-strung breeding by prancing and snorting and initially refusing to leave the other horses. Kenny, however, displayed some fine horsemanship and soon had Gandalf under control. She disappeared with a wave back down the trail.

Captain Gunn's chair was secured to the drop-down flap at the back of the wagon. Rocky joined the packhorse tied to the rear of the wagon. Captain Gunn had his water bottle, whisky flask, notebooks, and pencil handy, though it was unlikely he'd do much note taking. As the children passed the wagon on their way back to their position at the back of the herd with Gerry, he was already settling into the cushions for a nice long afternoon nap.

SHADOWS WERE LENGTHENING as the cattle drive reached its overnight stopping place. They had been steadily climbing for the past few hours, still following the course of the creek which was getting smaller and smaller the higher they got.

As the trail turned a corner, they could see that they were entering a small valley with a closed end and steep sides. It was a natural corral for the cattle, who spread out along both sides of the creek inside the valley and began to graze.

The children dismounted and reunited with Captain Gunn, who descended from the wagon refreshed by his nap and the easy and comfortable ride he had enjoyed all afternoon.

Joe came over to them.

"You're going to hobble your horses after they are untacked," he said, dangling a bunch of what looked like leather handcuffs connected by chains from one enormous fist. "It doesn't hurt the horses," he added, seeing Posy's worried look. "It just means they will stay close and won't wander too far. Look, I'll show you on the packhorse."

He untied the spare horse from the back of the wagon, took off his packsaddle, and proceeded to attach the cuffs to the horse's front feet. The horse didn't seem to mind and wandered slowly away, restricted in movement by a short length of light chain now stretched between his front feet.

Everyone attended to their horses in the same way, and then went to help Wee Tan with the baggage. He was busy with a couple of the cowboys, building a firepit and gathering fuel to cook the evening's meal.

"You take your bedrolls and find a good camping spot," said the cook, affectionately called "Cookie" by the regular cowboys. The children felt he deserved a great deal of respect for the tremendous job he did looking after everyone and only ever called him "Mr. Tan."

They dragged their bedrolls away from the wagon to a lovely spot beneath some trees with a vista over the rangeland back the way they'd come. They gathered some pine boughs to soften their beds and then decided to do a bit of exploring before dinner.

"Let's climb up for a better view," said Captain Gunn.

The children turned to look at him. When did Captain Gunn ever voluntarily take exercise of any sort, particularly when it involved climbing up a very steep hill? What was he up to?

The whole gang headed up the left-hand side of the small valley. As they got higher, they could see the camp below them, the cattle and the cowboys spread out across the valley. Leticia took a picture.

They had almost reached the crest of the hill, when Molly, who had taken the lead, gave a yell.

"Gosh, what on earth is this?" she exclaimed as the others panted up behind her.

They were on a small plateau slightly below the highest point of the valley wall. At the back of the plateau was a pile of rocks with a gaping dark opening partially covered by two signs that said, "Keep Out" and "Bad Air." In front of the entrance, among the rocks, were piles of discarded tools, wooden boxes, some broken and handleless pots, various bits of what looked like horse harness, and empty and rusty food tins.

"Thought so," said Captain Gunn. "This is an old mine. I had a feeling we might come across something like this on our ride across to Fintry. These sort of mines are often found in hillsides like this one, or so my reading tells me."

He warned them not to go near the entrance, and they poked around among the rubbish.

"It's pretty obvious this mine is abandoned," he said. "Not sure what they dug out of here and how long it's been like this. We'll ask Joe—he knows this area like the back of his hand and will have an idea what this is all about."

"Gosh, maybe it's a gold mine and we'll find another load of gold," said Mark imagining a splendid addition to his already spectacular train set, purchased with his share of the reward money from Brother XII's treasure.

Captain Gunn laughed. "Don't think we'll be so lucky twice in a lifetime. Those old miners knew a thing or two and would only have abandoned a claim once they were pretty sure it was all played out. Although, you never know," he finished, looking thoughtfully at the mine.

A short while later they could see the smoke from the cook fire and headed back down the hill. There was nothing like a day in the saddle (or in Captain Gunn's case, half a day) to work up a tremendous appetite.

WEE TAN HAD an ingenious arrangement for transporting fresh food; otherwise the diet on a cattle drive would have consisted of beans, rice, coffee, and not much else.

In the back of the wagon, installed down one side, was a large wooden box. Inside the box was another, smaller box, and the space between the two was lined with tightly packed hay. In the bottom of the smaller box wooden slats were laid across blocks of ice, and on top of the slats was a fine selection of food, including meat, cheese, butter, and eggs. There was a small opening that went through both boxes and led out of a hole in the bed of the wagon allowing melted ice to drain away.

"If I'm careful about not opening the box too often," said Wee Tan. "The ice won't melt for about five days. Designed the box myself and the cowboys all love me, I can tell you!"

Indeed, the meal Wee Tan produced was of the very finest cowboy variety. Sausages, canned beans, and bread baked that morning was finished off with delicious cake squares filled with dates and raisins. The cowboys drank cool bottles of beer, and Wee Tan had brought cola along for the children, though there hadn't been room in the cool box for more than one day's supply. From now on they would have to drink water from the water barrel.

When dinner was over the children helped Wee Tan and his daily assigned cowboy assistant to wash the dishes in the creek.

"You English kids are very polite—not like some I know," Wee Tan said.

He found the children's willingness to help with chores very refreshing, but Posy was his favourite. She was the age that his youngest child had been when he left China twenty years ago. Although he received letters and photographs from his wife back in China, he hadn't seen any of his family in all that time. He sent money back to China and was saving up to bring his family over, but it would be several more years before they were all reunited.

The clean-up crew returned to the campsite and found spots around the fire. Captain Gunn sat himself down beside Joe and offered him a drink from his silver flask.

"Do you know anything about that abandoned mine up the hill?" he asked as he filled his pipe in preparation for his post dinner smoke and whisky.

"Yes, a bit," said Joe, accepting a drink. "There are several abandoned silver mines around these parts. Some produced quite a lot, but it all ran out a decade or more ago. The miners moved on to greener pastures. There's nothing left but a bunch of garbage, certainly no more silver."

The cowboys were lounging on the ground smoking. Just as the children joined them, Gerry appeared from the direction of the parked wagon, carrying the banjo case they had seen loaded on the wagon back at the Quilchena.

"Know any cowboy songs?" he asked as he settled himself on a log.

"No," said Molly, locating and fixing Norm with a hard stare, "but we *do* know lots of pirate songs."

Norm turned pale and looked like he wanted to throw up.

"Well, how about I teach you one of mine, and you can teach me one of yours?" Gerry said as he got the banjo out of its case and started to tune it up. He strummed a few chords and then started to sing in a surprisingly clear and tuneful tenor:

Oh give me a home, where the buffalo roam
And the deer and the antelope play
Where seldom is heard a discouraging word
And the skies are not cloudy all day.

The cowboys joined in with the chorus.

Home, home on the range
Where the deer and the antelope play
Where seldom is heard a discouraging word
And the skies are not cloudy all day.

After a couple more verses the children got the hang of it and started singing the chorus along with the cowboys. By the last round, they were all singing loudly enough to scare away any wild animals that might have been lurking nearby.

Robert, one of the English mud pups, was seated near the group of children.

"Do you know the origin of cowboy songs?" he asked.

"No," said Harriet. "Do tell us."

"Well, you might hear singing through the night. There will always be two of us riding in opposite directions around the herd. We take it in turns, and it keeps the herd together and warns off the bears and cougars. It's a very old cowboy tradition."

"That's great," said Captain Gunn, squinting in the deepening dusk as he scribbled in his notebook. "It'll be an interesting fact to put in the book."

Molly asked if she could teach the group a pirate song. After singing a couple of verses, Gerry picked up the tune on his banjo, and soon cowboys and explorers alike were belting out Molly's favourite song.

Fifteen men on the dead man's chest—
... Yo-ho-ho, and a bottle of rum!
Drink and the devil had done for the rest—
... Yo-ho-ho, and a bottle of rum!

The mate was fixed by the bos'n's pike
The bos'n' brained with a markin spike
And Cookey's throat was marked belike

It had been gripped by fingers ten.
And there they lay all good dead men

Like break o' day in a boozing ken
Yo-ho-ho and a bottle of rum.

The choice of song was no accident. Molly and the rest of the crew had sung it constantly on their sailing adventure two years earlier. It became a fitting anthem when, partway through that trip, they encountered *actual* pirates—including a certain fair-haired one who had seemed just as out of place on the *Black Pearl* as he did now, sitting a few feet away surrounded by cheerful cowboys.

Most of the group gathered around the fire had no idea that Molly's song had a hidden meaning. Only Sophie noticed Norm's increasing discomfort, as he seemed to shrink under the weight of his cowboy hat. She thought he looked distinctly hunted. Sophie still wasn't sure if Norm could be trusted, but she knew that he didn't stand a chance against Molly.

LATER THAT NIGHT, Molly passed Norm on her way to the wagon for a snack and decided to seize her chance and confront him directly. But before she could say anything, Norm surprised her by speaking up for the first time.

"Please, miss," he stammered, "I've done my time and I'm going straight. Please, please leave me alone."

Molly wished the others were around to witness his admission of guilt. Unmoved by his plea, she hissed, "You may have done your time, but time hasn't erased the scar of what your nasty friend did to me." She rolled up her sleeve to reveal what had been a bullet hole but was now nothing more a tiny pink pucker mark. Still, her dramatic words filled Norm with overwhelming terror and guilt.

"You'd better watch out," she threatened. "I've got my eye on you, and so do all my friends. One wrong move and you'll be back behind bars so quickly you won't even know how you got there."

With that, she turned on her heel and swept back to camp to tell the others about her confrontation. When she got there, she found Sophie trying to round up everyone, including Captain Gunn, to brush their teeth. After she recounted her tale (adding a few details for effect), the reaction was less enthusiastic than she had hoped.

"So..." Captain Gunn began, "what you're telling us, Molly, is that young Norm declared that he was trying to turn his life around, begged you to stop hounding him, and in response you threatened to send him back to jail?"

"Well, yes," said Molly. "But you're missing the point! We now know for certain that he was part of the *Black Pearl* gang. He admitted it! He said he did time for it! That should be enough to get him fired—at least!"

Harriet, not usually one to speak up, cleared her throat. "It seems to me," she began, "that once you 'do time' for a crime, and you get out of jail, it's like the law's way of saying now you get to start over."

"Yes," chimed in Mark. "It's like when I ate all the biscuits that were to be served at Mother's ladies' luncheon last spring, and as punishment I had to stay in my room with no dessert all weekend. Once the weekend was over, I was allowed to eat biscuits again. Imagine if I was forbidden from eating biscuits for the rest of my life!"

Molly rolled her eyes. "We're not talking about some stupid biscuits here, Mark. We're talking about pirates! Pirates with guns!"

"Now, Molly," said Captain Gunn in a calm voice. "No one here is comparing biscuit theft to you getting shot. Believe me, that was one of the most frightening days of my long life! But Harriet and Mark have a point. In the eyes of the law, Norm has made up for his wrongdoings. He's free to live his life like anyone else. And it sounds to me like he is truly sorry. I would strongly suggest that you stop provoking him."

"I agree, Molly," said Sophie. "I was watching Norm tonight during the pirate song, and he looked positively ill. Whatever bad things he's done in the past, it's obvious he feels terrible. And I don't think you realize the effect you have on people sometimes."

Molly felt a tiny twinge of guilt at Sophie's last statement, which she knew was not only about her behaviour towards Norm but also about her teasing of Sophie. But mostly, she was annoyed that everyone seemed to be taking Norm's side. Why did Norm's feelings matter more than hers? She still believed that a leopard never changed its spots, no matter what everyone else said.

They could hear the murmur of the cowboys round the fire, which was slowing dying down to glowing embers. Slowly the children made their way to bed, lying on their backs and gazing at the sky. There was no moon and the stars shone brightly. Captain Gunn and Mark tried to pick out the constellations, but they gave up after finding the Big Dipper. It was obvious that everyone had other things on their mind that night.

THREE DAYS LATER, the cattle drive wound its way down a track from the high country they had just crossed. The second night they had camped beside a small lake, fringed in rushes. The cattle and horses had to wade knee deep through mud to get to the water. The third night they camped beside another creek, but this time there was no handy valley to contain the cattle, and the nightriders had a hard job keeping wanderers close to the herd. For a couple of hours after breakfast, Posy, Robert, and George helped round up the stragglers.

The guest cowpokes had settled into the rhythm of the days, and even Captain Gunn appeared fitter and keener. He now sometimes got back on Rocky after a post-lunch nap in the wagon and rode with the rest of them for a couple of hours.

Mid-afternoon of the fourth day since leaving the Douglas Lake Ranch, they left the high country and in the direction of Okanagan Lake, although they could see no sign of it. The track they followed became narrower and narrower, until the cattle moved single file and Wee Tan's wagon came dangerously close to dropping off into the gulch and creek below. Finally the trail widened and broke out of the trees and they found themselves in paradise. The children stopped their horses and gazed in wonder. They had entered a small, perfectly oval valley. The creek widened out and meandered across the middle of the valley, and instead of the brown rangeland they had grown accustomed to, the grass was lush and green. Over to the left, on the other side of the valley, they caught a glimpse of a house, surrounded by an orchard and gardens. Midway along the valley the creek swelled into a small lake, which then narrowed again at its farthest end and fell over a small waterfall.

"Leticia, take a photograph," said Harriet. "I'd like a copy of that one to put into my journal. Look, we'll all line up and you can get us in the foreground."

Gerry rode ahead. The children really no longer needed a chaperone, but from Gerry's point of view it was a lot easier looking after them than doing his regular cowboy job. Leticia lined everyone up then shot a couple of photos, one with the gang and another just of the valley.

They cantered over to join the rest of the cattle drive. The cattle did their usual when freed from being driven forwards and settled down to graze the lush grass or stand in the creek taking a drink. Wee Tan, who had been just behind them, pulled his wagon into the shade of a grove of aspen trees close to the creek.

Sam rode over.

"We're going to spend the rest of the day here, and then head down to Fintry in the morning. Lovely spot—you can swim in the lake if you like."

They did like, and soon after tending to their horses they were splashing in the shallow lake. They could hardly believe that the cattle drive was almost over and that after delivering the cattle to the dock at Fintry, they would be heading back to the Douglas Lake Ranch. Sam said a truck from Fintry would give them a ride the following afternoon to the O'Keefe Ranch, twenty miles away at the head of Okanagan Lake. They were invited to stay overnight with Tierney O'Keefe and his wife and then a truck from the DLR would come and pick them. The drive back to the ranch would take four hours as opposed to the four days it had taken on horseback. After spending a final night at the ranch as the Wards' guests (where Posy was hoping for her much anticipated ride on Gandalf), they would be picked up by Mr. Schwimmer and returned to the Quilchena in preparation for their trip back down to the coast.

Sam had also explained that once the cattle were delivered to the barge at Fintry, he and the other cowboys would ride, leading the extra horses, along the west side of Okanagan Lake to the O'Keefe Ranch. There they would pick up another herd of cows and calves and drive them as far as a ranch in the small community of Westwold, before striking off on the road that ran from Westwold back to the DLR. He and the other cowboys would have ridden a huge circle.

AFTER THEIR SWIM the children did a bit of exploring. They found wooden irrigation channels leading from the creek into the valley, which explained why the valley was so green. Old log buildings dotted the expanse, one housing a number of goats. After their walk, they joined Captain Gunn, who was lazing in the shade of an aspens.

"I've just realized I'm going to have to say goodbye to Spotty tomorrow," said Posy, looking very glum.

"It might not be goodbye forever," said Captain Gunn munching on a snack cadged off the obliging Wee Tan. "We'll be staying back at the Quilchena for a couple of nights before we take the train down to Vancouver, and if Sam and the other cowboys get back before we leave for the coast, I'm sure you'll be able to go out for a ride."

"I suppose so," said Posy, "but it won't be the same. There might even be other children staying at the hotel who want to ride him. It's been like having my own pony, and I don't want anyone else to ride him."

Posy was after all only ten years old, and the concept of permanent partings from things she loved was new to her. Parting from Spotty was going to be hard, but she was determined to put on a brave face.

"What are we going to do when we get back to Vancouver?" asked Molly. "I know it's at least three weeks before we have to be back in Quebec City to catch the ship home."

"Not sure about that," said Captain Gunn. "Lots to see and do around Vancouver."

He was being vague, and the children knew him well enough to know that this meant he was planning something fun. But whatever it was, he wouldn't reveal it until he was good and ready.

It was their last night with the cowboys, and Wee Tan prepared a wonderful farewell feast: steaks from the bottom of the cooler, fried onions and mushrooms, fried potatoes, and boiled carrots. For dessert they picked plums that grew wild in the valley.

After dinner everyone sat round and reminisced about the drive and how much fun it had been for a bunch of rookie English children. Joe and Sam said some very nice things about them, and the cowboys gave them a rousing three cheers. Gerry brought his banjo out again and as dusk settled across the valley, he played and everyone sang. Cowboy love songs, cowboy sad songs, cowboy funny songs. Someone began to sing the pirate song Molly had taught the cowboys on their first night, but this time Molly didn't use it as an opportunity to torture Norm. She still didn't trust the timid cowboy, but scaring the wits out of him wasn't doing any good. If he did something shady—which she was sure he would sooner or later—she would be watching him. Closely.

CHAPTER SEVEN
FINTRY

The sun slid up over the top of the hills across Okanagan Lake, finding its way into the little valley where cowboys and children still slept. The rays hit Posy directly, and she turned her head away and murmured in her sleep. She had been dreaming of her and Spotty riding into a huge stadium with searchlights picking them out as they cantered around the ring.

"Whoa, Spotty," she mumbled before sitting upright in her sleeping bag and looking around her in some confusion. She wasn't in a stadium; she was in a quiet valley in the heart of British Columbia and today was her last day with her beloved pony.

The human participants in the cattle drive slept on, lumps in their sleeping rolls, some around the campfire, some under the wagon, and the English contingent in a pleasantly secluded spot under a stand of trees.

Posy wriggled out of her sleeping bag, pulled on her jeans and boots, and looked around for the horses. Sam had decreed that the horses had such lush grass to graze on that they would be unlikely to wander far, so they had been turned out without their customary hobbles, and Posy could see them peacefully grazing here and there. She found Spotty near the creek and decided that she would catch him and give him a very special grooming.

Moving quietly so as not to disturb anyone, she crept over to the wagon, stepping over a couple of cowboys to reach the rack of halters hanging on the side and the communal box of grooming equipment that lived under the driver's seat.

Spotty saw her coming, and with a gentle nicker he ambled over to Posy and put his nose into the halter. He knew that Posy always had a treat for him, and he wasn't disappointed as the little girl fished out a couple of dusty sugar lumps from the pocket of her jeans.

Soon the pony was tied to a tree branch and enjoying a thorough grooming. Posy brushed him until he shone and her arms ached. She combed his mane and tail until every hair was separated and stirred in the gentle breeze that was finding its way into the valley.

Posy stepped back to admire her handiwork and felt the tears pricking behind her eyes. How could she bear to be parted from her Spotty? If only England wasn't so far away—she could have bought him with her share of the reward money from Brother XII's treasure. She hadn't spent a penny of it yet. But of course, despite Posy's young age, she was mature enough to know that her dream was impossible and she was going to have to part with Spotty by the end of the day, once the cattle were delivered to Fintry.

Posy dashed the tears away, straightened her shoulders, and decided to make the best of things. She would have another day to ride Spotty and then she would try to say goodbye without making a fuss.

She turned away from the pony and saw that Wee Tan was kindling the cooking fire and starting to get breakfast ready. He signalled her over and handed her a piece of chocolate.

"You look like you need a treat," he said, smiling down at her. "Don't you worry about Spotty. He's a favourite back at the Quilchena and gets spoiled by all the cowboys."

Posy thanked him and headed back over to the others, who were now in various stages of waking up. Days on the trail, good food, and late nights around the campfire meant they all slept well, now used to sleeping outside with nothing between them and the stars.

BY 10:00 A.M. the cattle drive was ready for the last leg of the journey—at least for the English participants. The cattle had been rounded up. With the cowboys on both flanks of the herd, and the children, Captain Gunn, and Wee Tan bringing up the rear, the whole gang began heading along the road that led downhill out of the valley.

Posy glanced behind her as Sam gave the order to move on out and saw that the beautiful valley was once again quiet and empty. It really was a little piece of paradise and Posy would never forget the time they had spent there, short as it had been. She gave Spotty a squeeze with her legs, taking her place in line with the other children and Captain Gunn.

THE ROAD RAN beside the creek, which plunged down into a gully. They could see it below them to their right through the pine trees, and the road ran parallel but high on the side of the gully. It was easy moving the cattle, as they had nowhere to go except forward. It didn't take long before the road came out of the trees and met another road that ran along the huge lake. It was their first sight of Okanagan Lake, and it did not disappoint them. The lake stretched north and south and they could not see either end. They could, however, see across it to the hills on the other side, and Molly could make a good guess at the location of the airport, near the town of Vernon. The waters of the lake were dotted with boats of all descriptions. It looked like a wonderful summer playground, but the cowboys were not here to play—they still had a job to do. The herd turned to the right, followed the main road for half a mile or so, and then turned again to the left and headed down the hill. The road followed a series of switchbacks, and below them they could see a vast area of flat land that bordered the lake.

Sam rode back to them and filled them in on their destination.

"You're going to enjoy meeting Captain James Dun-Waters," he said. "English, like you, or rather Scottish. Fintry is named after his estate back in Scotland. He's a wonder, I can tell you. Turned this place into an incredibly productive farm. Prize cattle and orchards, mainly, but a smattering of everything else. The place is a hive of activity. People around here call him the Laird of Fintry, and I'd say he richly deserves that title. After we've got the cattle down to the beach to meet the barge, you are all invited to lunch with him and his wife at the Manor House."

The Manor House? What kind of place here in the wilds of British Columbia could possibly be called a manor house? Maybe it was a joke, and they would find that the grandly named building was really just a log cabin.

The road straightened out as it reached the bottom of the hill and the cowboys rode out along the flanks of the herd to keep them contained. They passed an extraordinary circular barn on their left, various other farm buildings, and seemingly endless rows of fruit trees, before the road finally ended at the lake. After the cattle were driven into a large pen close to the wharf, Joe closed the gate on them with a flourish and gave a huge "Whoopee!" They had successfully driven the cattle across forty miles of difficult terrain without losing a single one.

There was a large shed on the edge of the lake next to the wharf. As everyone dismounted a man emerged from the shed and came over to greet them.

The Laird of Fintry presented a striking and eccentric figure. He was dressed in a tweed three-piece suit with plus fours, a white shirt and tie, polished brown brogues, and a beret with a brooch and feather. He looked fairly old, but he walked with authority and without the use of a cane.

"Welcome to Fintry," he boomed in a broad Scottish accent. "I see you all made it in one piece—that's quite a ride you've had.

I'm Captain James Cameron Dun-Waters, but I'm generally called J.C. by my friends, and I can see we're all going to be great friends!"

Everyone introduced themselves, and at Sam's suggestion they watered the horses in the lake, loosened their girths, and tied them to a fence.

"Just leave your bags over there," said the Laird, pointing to a spot under a tree. "You're coming to lunch with me and then we'll come back and pick up your luggage with the truck. My foreman is going to drive you along the lake to the O'Keefe Ranch."

The English gang turned to Sam and Joe and the other cowboys. This was goodbye. After the barge had arrived and they had loaded the cattle the cowboys were heading to the O'Keefe themselves, but on horseback, not by truck. It was a distance of some twenty miles, and they planned to camp one night along the way. The children and Captain Gunn would have left the O'Keefe by the time the cowboys reached there, so it really was goodbye for now. They weren't sure if they would see them at Quilchena before leaving for the coast, as it would depend on how long the next phase of the cattle drive took and how long Captain Gunn decided to stay at the hotel before heading down to the coast.

Posy went over to Spotty and flung her arms around his neck.

"Just in case I don't see you again, you're the best pony in the whole world."

Spotty nuzzled Posy looking for treats and was rewarded by a whole handful of sugar lumps provided by Wee Tan. With a last look back, Posy joined the others, who had said less emotional goodbyes to their own mounts. Molly, in particular, was more than happy to have completed the cattle drive, but had decided that if she never went riding again it wouldn't bother her in the slightest.

The Laird led the way along a neatly gravelled path, through a grove of trees and onto a wide, green lawn edged with glorious rose bushes in full bloom. The entire crew stopped and gazed in awe at the house in front of them.

It looked as if it had been transported piece by piece from England and reassembled in this most splendid of settings. The fact that it was built mostly of rock, rather than the wood generally used in other buildings, including the massive Quilchena Hotel, made it look like a grand English (or Scottish) manor house. In fact, the Laird told them, as they stood gazing at it in admiration, it *was* actually called the Manor House. Surrounding the house were velvet green lawns, immaculately maintained shrubs and the beautiful rose garden. They could see the sparkling blue waters of the lake lapping up to the edge of the gardens. How on earth had this gracious manor house been constructed on the edge of the wilderness?

They crossed the lawn and mounted the stone steps to a wide veranda. Molly and Mark were first up the steps and almost knocked Sophie, who was just behind them, down the steps as they backed away from a giant bear who was standing on his hind legs beside the front door.

The Laird laughed at their consternation and coming up the steps, patted the bear on his nose.

"I keep him here to scare my drinking buddies into sobering up after an evening of whisky and cards!" he laughed. "Shot him myself up in the Yukon, twenty years ago. I'll show you the rest of my hunting trophies after lunch."

As they entered the house a lady came forward to welcome them.

"Meet Margaret, my wife," said the Laird. "Here's a bunch of English explorers who've been surviving on camp food for the last few days. Hope you've got something good for lunch."

Margaret smiled and greeted Captain Gunn and the children.

"Perhaps you'd like to wash up before lunch," she said.

Sophie hoped they didn't look too disreputable. As she glanced in a huge mirror in the hallway, she realized that her standards of cleanliness had taken a break, and in fact they did all look pretty grubby.

They took turns using an enormous bathroom floored in marble and equipped with a pile of fluffy towels, which Sophie was rather afraid looked less than pristine after the whole gang had done their best to wash off the trail dirt accumulated over the past few days.

They sat down to lunch in a beautiful dining room, panelled in fine inlaid wood and boasting a huge fireplace and massive paintings, which filled most of the wall space. The floors were covered in gorgeous Persian carpets, and lunch was served on fine china, with solid silver cutlery and crystal glasses.

Over lunch the Laird told them a little about his estate.

"Came here in 1909," he began, "and I've built it up into one of Canada's finest farms. I've got a prize herd of Ayrshire cows— you've probably noticed the circular barn I had designed especially for them. I win prizes all over the place with them. I hear that you came down through the valley we call the High Farm. That's part of my estate and it's where I grow the hay for my cattle."

Captain Gunn was, of course, fascinated by the Laird's history and the extent of his endeavours. Molly could see that he was already thinking about making the Laird the subject of a book. The Laird told them that he generated his own electricity from the same creek that they had camped beside the night before, which after leaving the High Farm valley, tumbled down over a series of waterfalls. He also had a telephone system to communicate between the various farm buildings and the Manor House. All in all it was extraordinary to have created a self-contained community on the edge of the wilderness.

The talk turned to future plans, and the Laird told them that at the age of seventy-four he felt it was time to retire.

"I've just signed over the entire estate, except this house, to an organization called Fairbridge Farms Training Schools. They bring underprivileged children from England and give them an education, as well as training them in farm management. The first group just arrived last month, and I think some of them are finding this place a bit hard to get used to. Most come from very poor backgrounds back in England, and some of them have never even seen a cow!"

After lunch, the Laird had one more thing to show them. They followed him out of the dining room and down a couple of steps into a room that was crammed with the fruits of his many years as a big game hunter. The exhibits included a moose, several mountain sheep, and two massively antlered deer. Posy thought killing all these animals simply to hang on someone's wall was cruel. She quietly left the room to wait on the veranda so she wouldn't have to look at the trophies anymore. She hoped the Laird wouldn't think she was rude.

In pride of place, and displayed in a grotto constructed of great jagged rocks, was a grizzly bear. The bear on the veranda looked quite tame compared with this specimen. Standing with his great jaws wide and with the huge hump on his shoulders emphasising his reputation as a fearsome predator, the bear gazed at the group of children with malevolence.

"Perhaps it's just as well we haven't met one of those in the wild," said Mark as he stood beside the bear. He only reached to the creature's shoulder.

The tour ended and the party moved back to the veranda as a farm truck drew up at the side of the house.

"Right, pile in," said the Laird. "Bill here will take you over to pick up your luggage and then drive you up the lake to the O'Keefe, where you're expected for dinner. You'll be pleased to know that and you'll be sleeping in proper beds tonight. I think they are sending a truck over from Douglas Lake to pick you up sometime tomorrow. Not much happens round here that I don't know about!"

The children and Captain Gunn said their goodbyes and thank yous to the Laird and his wife and climbed into the back of the pickup truck, which drove the short distance back to the wharf.

"Oh, look!" said Posy. "They haven't left yet. Spotty's still there!"

There was a barge tied up to the wharf and the cowboys were just loading the last of the cattle on board. The horses were still tied up in the shade.

"You've said your goodbyes," said Sophie to Posy. "Come on, we don't want to keep Bill waiting. We'd better just grab out stuff and get back in the truck."

Reluctantly, Posy turned her back on the horses, and went with the others over to their pile of belongings.

Leticia was the first to notice something was wrong.

"Where's my camera?" she asked. "I know I left it beside my saddlebag. I took it out to snap a photo of the end of the cattle drive and forgot to bring it when we went for lunch."

The saddlebags were not as they had left them, piled neatly under a tree. They were lying scattered about with the flaps open and various bits and pieces tossed into the nearby undergrowth.

Captain Gunn bent over his bag and slowly stood up with a white face.

"My notebooks have gone," he said. "All the research I've done since arriving at the Quilchena, every bit of information I've gathered about my book—gone! Without them I can't write my book. They're irreplaceable."

Everyone had seen Captain Gunn scribbling in a series of notebooks he carried with him everywhere he went. They could appreciate the enormity of the loss.

Each of the children had lost something. Even Sophie's first-aid kit was missing.

Captain Gunn hurried over to where Sam and Joe were supervising the last cattle to board the barge. The cowboys began to look around the area where the horses were tied, questioning the other cowboys who were getting their horses ready to leave.

Joe came over to the group with a grim face.

"Norm and his horse are missing," he said. "That's pretty suspicious. I don't want to accuse anyone without firm evidence, but we need to find him and ask him if he knows anything about this."

"Of course he knows about this!" exclaimed Molly. "He's a hardened criminal! We know him from the last time we were in Canada, and he was involved with a very nasty gang. He's even been in jail!"

She rolled up her sleeve to show Joe and Sam her scar. "You need firm evidence? Here it is!"

The two men were taken aback by Molly's outburst, though they couldn't really see what it had to do with the tiny pink mark on her arm. Sam turned to Captain Gunn.

"Mr. Cameron, is this . . . could this be true?"

"Unfortunately, yes," Captain Gunn admitted. "Molly recognized Norm as soon as she saw him. He was part of the gang that attacked us two years ago. Although he wasn't the one who shot Molly. I thought he seemed harmless, and since he had paid his dues to society and seemed to be making an honest go of things, well... I'm sorry to say I discouraged Molly from saying anything to you."

There was an awkward silence. Molly felt totally vindicated, but she knew now was not the right time to do an "I told you so" dance. The other children felt varying degrees of shock and disappointment. Like Captain Gunn, they had come to believe that Norm couldn't hurt a fly and that Molly was being unfair to judge him so harshly. Now it seemed that Molly was right—a leopard really didn't change his spots. Not only that, but this leopard had taken off with some of their prized possessions!

Captain Gunn was pacing back and forth, and had now turned a beetroot shade of red. He was dashing the sweat from his brow and muttering incoherently, although the others caught a word here and there.

"Scoundrel, wastrel, crook, rascal, rat," were some of the words that seemed to issue from Captain Gunn on puffs of steam. To say he was angry doesn't tell the tale. He was incandescent with rage, and Sophie began to worry again about heart attacks.

Finally he came to a halt in front on Joe, Sam, and the children.

"We'll just have to chase him. He can't have gone that far. Come on, you lot," he said, pointing at the children. "Get ready to ride after him."

Posy's heart gave a leap of joy. She was going to ride Spotty again! But before she could make a move over to the line of horses, Sam held up his hand.

"Sorry, Mr. Cameron, but that's not going to happen. You are expected at the O'Keefe Ranch this evening, and besides that I can't spare anyone to go back with you, and you're certainly not going on your own."

Unfortunately for Sam, he had never before come up against Captain Gunn's formidable will. The argument raged back and forth, but eventually the inevitable happened—Sam gave in.

"Okay," he said, "I suppose I really couldn't stop you if you decided to jump on your horses and take off, so it'd be better if we do this in an organized fashion. Bill," he said, calling to the man who had driven them over from the ranch house, "can you tell the Laird what's happened and that you won't be driving this lot to the O'Keefe Ranch, after all? Ask him to give Mr. O'Keefe a call and tell him he won't be having any house guests this evening."

Sam stood in thought for a few moments and then started issuing orders.

"Wee Tan," he called to the cook who was resting on the drop-down board on the back of the cook wagon. "Can you fix up a parcel of food that will keep our guests alive for a few days?"

Wee Tan sprang into action and pulled out bags and cans from his wagon. Sam called one of the cowboys over and asked him to bring over the spare packhorse.

"You're going to need Louis here to carry your food and bed-rolls. You need to watch very carefully while we saddle him. It's quite an art saddling and packing stuff on one of these saddles."

Molly, although not desperately keen on more riding, was very keen indeed at the idea of chasing the villainous Norm and recovering their stolen property. She and Leticia watched carefully as Sam took them through the saddling and packing of the docile pack horse, Louis, who up to this point had spend his days ambling along tied to the back of the cook wagon.

Sophie talked to Wee Tan. She had watched him cooking, and it had seemed miraculous what he could produce from the various sacks of dried goods, tins, and some fresh food from the cooler. One of the children's favourites had been the bannock bread that Wee Tan had made fresh every day. A mixture of flour, salt, oil, and water, it wasn't much like the fresh bread they were used to, but was very tasty when cooked in a skillet over the campfire.

"Not too much in the way of fresh food left," said the estimable cook. "But I've packed some basic supplies. It's just too bad you won't get to taste my cousin's cooking. He's the cook at the O'Keefe Ranch and he turns out some pretty good chow, I can tell you."

Sam had been thinking about where Norm might have gone and came up with a theory.

"We can't be sure, but I have a feeling he might have headed back the way we came. He would know he'd be spotted if he headed along the road towards the O'Keefe, and he's not likely to hang around here.

"I'll tell you what. We'll all mount up together and go as far as the turn off up to the High Farm. Thomas and Charlie are pretty good trackers. We'll put them in front and see if they can see any tracks heading back up the road towards where we camped last night."

Posy was reunited with Spotty, and the others reclaimed their mounts and tied on their saddlebags containing the remains of their personal possessions. The whole gang of English children, Captain Gunn, and cowboys started back up the road out of Fintry. The cattle drive was over, but the adventure was not.

CHAPTER EIGHT
CHASING NORM

Thomas and Charlie walked ahead of the others, leading their horses and looking down at the dirt road. Occasionally they stopped and knelt down, looking carefully at the hoof prints that covered the road.

"There's been a horse going back along the road here," said Charlie. "Doesn't take much of a tracker to figure that out!"

At the point where the road to the High Farm met the road that headed north up the west side of Okanagan Lake towards the O'Keefe Ranch, Thomas and Charlie scouted carefully in the dirt.

"See here?" said Thomas. "There are fresh prints on top of all the tracks made by the cattle and us when we headed down. I'm pretty sure there's been a horse going back up this road in the last hour or so."

"That's enough for me," said Captain Gunn. "Many thanks for your help, all of you. Hope to see you back at the Quilchena."

"Hold your horses!" said Sam. "Do you think you can remember your way back? Nothing looks the same when you're going the other way."

"I've got my compass in my pocket," said Mark. "Lucky I didn't have it in my saddlebag. I'm pretty sure if we head due west and follow the trail, we'll end up back where we started."

"All right," said Sam, "I don't like it, but I can see you're set on going. The O'Keefe has a telephone and when we get there tomorrow, we'll call ahead to the Quilchena and Douglas Lake. I'll suggest they send out a search party from their end so either you'll find them or they'll find you. I don't think Norm is too clever, and I can't really see that he would have any other idea than to head back over the range. Not sure what he thinks he'll do when he gets there, but I don't think he's doing much thinking right now."

Captain Gunn was in a tearing hurry to get back on the trail, so goodbyes and good lucks were said quickly and the English cowpokes headed back up the road to the High Farm. They were now on their own, without the experienced backcountry horsemen to guide them and get them out of any scrapes they might encounter. Sophie watched the cowboys disappear up the road towards the north end of the lake and wished she were going with them. She thought wistfully of the O'Keefe Ranch, with its civilized meals, baths, and beds. She also wasn't sure how good she would be in creating edible meals out of the basic supplies they now had, but she would do her best.

Louis, the packhorse, was not the fastest horse in the herd, so their speed was limited. He seemed to like Harriet's horse, Jake, the best, so Harriet took the lead rope and led him from her saddle.

Getting organized for this unexpected trip had taken some time, and it was nearly evening by the time they emerged from the wooded road and into the High Farm valley. Captain Gunn wanted to keep going, but Sophie pointed out that this was a good place to camp and that Norm wouldn't be doing much riding after dusk. He didn't know he was being followed so probably wasn't riding at top speed. In any case, she said, everyone needed to eat and rest.

They picked a pleasant spot by the little lake and soon had the horses hobbled and their gear on the patient Louis unpacked. They gathered wood for a fire, and Sophie created a basic dinner of rice, a tin of beans, and some of Wee Tan's bannock made that morning. They finished the meal off with plums from the nearby trees, and Captain Gunn had some whisky and lit his evening pipe. It had been a long and eventful day, and before long everyone was yawning.

Sophie, who was in her most adult-like mood, ordered one and all to bed. Soon Captain Gunn was snoring and Harriet, Mark, Leticia, and Posy were fast asleep. Only Sophie and Molly remained awake. Sophie could feel the tension in the air and decided to bring things out in the open.

"You know, Molly, I'm really sorry. That is, I think we're all really sorry that we didn't believe you about Norm being up to no good."

Molly paused, a bit surprised by Sophie's apology. They hadn't been on the best of terms all summer, and Molly knew that she was partly to blame for that.

"That's okay, Soph," Molly said. "I guess I understand why you wanted to see the good in him. So did I... after a while. I'm actually sorry my first instinct about him was so spot on."

Sophie snorted, which was very unlike her. "Really? You wanted to be wrong? I never thought I'd hear you say that."

Molly laughed. Then after a minute she said, "Soph?"

"Yes?"

"I'm sorry I made fun of you that day in front of those cowboys. I didn't mean to be cruel. Sometimes these things just come flying out of my mouth before I can stop them."

Sophie sighed. "I know. And I forgive you. Although I was really angry at you that day."

"If you were so cross, why didn't you say anything?"

"What could I say? Unlike you, I don't have the gift of always having the perfect insult to hurl at whoever has ticked me off."

"Oh, come on. I've seen you lose your temper before. Remember that time on the *South Islander*?"

"I only lose my temper after I've been bottling up my anger for days or weeks. Not like you—ready to have a go at anyone you think deserves it, right then and there."

Molly pondered that for a moment.

"Do you know what I just realized?" she asked.

"What?"

"It's an absolute miracle that you and I are friends after all these years. No, wait! That came out all wrong. What I meant is that we're so different in every possible way. Yet I couldn't imagine going on one of these adventures without you, Sophie. It just wouldn't be the same."

"It wouldn't be the same at all," Sophie deadpanned. "Without me reminding you to wash up, you'd be so dirty by the end of the trip your own mother wouldn't recognize you."

The girls laughed, and once they had stopped laughing they realized there was nothing left to say. Whatever tension had been building all summer long had eased. They fell asleep happy, knowing that although they may not be the sort of friends who had everything in common, they still shared a bond that could not be broken.

THE NEXT MORNING they struck camp, very careful to water down the fireplace and make sure they left no rubbish behind. They rode out of the valley without a backward glance, focused on the trail ahead. The first part was narrow and steep, and they went in single file, but once the trail widened they began looking left and right for any signs of Norm. Even without a compass the trail would be hard to miss. Two hundred fifty cattle, a wagon, and more than a dozen horses had left their mark, and they easily retraced their outward track. After a couple of hours of steady riding, Mark, who was riding a little ahead of the others, gave a shout and pointed off to one side. The others caught up with him and dismounted. Near a tiny creek they saw the remains of a campfire, which was still smoking. Beside the campfire they found an empty whisky bottle (obviously Norm did not limit himself to one glass of whisky a day, as Captain Gunn did) and a couple of opened cans that had contained food. Norm had left an untidy campsite, and it provided a clue as to how far ahead he was.

"From the heat left in the fireplace, I figure he's a couple of hours ahead of us," said Mark, who had become the gang's self-appointed tracking expert. "If we hurry we can catch up with him. Remember he doesn't know he's being followed."

They remounted and headed out along the trail. Molly and Posy set a cracking pace, but soon realized that there was a problem, or rather two problems. One was that Captain Gunn, although much improved as a rider, could not sustain a trot or canter for more than a few minutes. The other was that Louis, the packhorse, had a lazy personality, and Harriet, who was leading him, was getting frustrated.

"He keeps almost pulling me off backwards," she wailed, as she struggled to keep Louis going at the same pace as Jake.

Posy had an idea.

"Why not tie him to one of the rings on the back of the saddle?" she suggested. "Then Jake is taking his weight, not you. And how about cutting a switch from one of those trees over there, and tapping him on his backside to keep him moving."

Things went better after that, but still Captain Gunn could not go as fast as they would have liked. He was getting crosser and crosser and rode in silence with a grim look on his face. The loss of his notebooks was monumental, and if they didn't recover them, the whole trip would be wasted. Of course, he could have reconstructed some of his notes, but he had put down many ideas and tidbits of information from the cowboys and those would be hard to remember. Not to mention the descriptions of the trail, the campsites, words to cowboy songs—and on and on.

The others rode with their own thoughts. Molly was very keen on the chase and catching up with Norm. She wanted to have a serious talk with him.

Leticia really wanted her camera back. She had found the used film canisters in her pack, but the film still in the camera had some of her best shots, and the camera itself was a prized possession.

Mark was enjoying being back on the trail. He had really come a long way with his riding, and felt that being out in the wilderness was better than being polite and having a bath at the O'Keefe Ranch.

Sophie would much rather have been having a bath, as she now felt distinctly grubby. She had been looking forward to trying out a shower in the marble bathroom at the O'Keefe that Sam had described to her. Showers were practically unknown in England—everyone took baths and hair was washed with the aid of a large china jug kept on the edge of the bath. It was strange that such a modern convenience could be found so far away from civilization. She was also concerned about the kind of food they were now eating. It really was very basic, and even a couple of days without vegetables was not good for anyone.

Harriet, whose notebook had also gone missing, would have very much liked to get it back, but she was not too keen about more riding. She quite liked the thought of a few days in the luxury of the Quilchena, swimming and drawing in her book. She was also getting fed up with Louis, whose gait had improved somewhat, but for whom her irritation was developing into dislike.

Posy was the only one who was enjoying herself purely and simply because she was back on Spotty. This was an unexpected bonus of them all getting robbed, and she would quite happily have chased after Norm for weeks!

Late in the afternoon they stopped to rest beside a little lake where they could water the horses. They were now in the high country and the trail had been winding up, down and around hills and patches of forest. They were still clearly following the outgoing trail—finding their way was not the problem. The problem was catching up with Norm.

"Sam told me that we covered ten to twelve miles a day with the cattle, but that horses on their own could go twice that distance," said Leticia. "Norm is probably getting farther and farther in front of us, because we're not going as fast as real cowboys."

Here she glanced at Captain Gunn, who was reclining against a log and looking pretty glum.

"Yes, I know I'm a failure as a cowboy," he said with an attempt at humour. "I'm certainly appreciating the easy time I had of it on the way over with that lovely comfy chair in the back of the wagon."

"Perhaps we should split up," said Molly. "The fastest riders could go on ahead, and Uncle Bert and whoever is leading Louis can follow at their own pace."

"There is no way we are splitting up," said Sophie. "You never know what might happen up here miles from civilization. Finding Norm is not as important as staying safe."

"Well, I can't see what else we can do other than keep going," said Mark. "Maybe Norm will go through the stuff he stole and dump it beside the trail when he stops for the night. Or maybe Sam and Joe will send out a posse from the other end and they'll catch him before we do."

In the end they decided to keep going and finally stopped for the night as it was getting dusk. It had taken them four days to cross from the Douglas Lake Ranch to Fintry, and they figured they could make it all the way back in less than three. They had already been on the trail for a full day, and they thought they could make it back to their very first camp spot near the abandoned silver mine by the end of the next day.

THE INITIAL EXCITEMENT on being hot on the trail of Norm had long faded by the afternoon of the following day. All of them, with the possible exception of Posy, were now just enduring the endless hours in the saddle. They hadn't seen any more signs of Norm, who might, for all they knew, have branched off either to the north or the south. They were simply backtracking over the route they had taken just a few days earlier with the cattle drive.

Late in the afternoon they all perked up as they recognized the site of the silver mine camp. Regardless of where Norm was, they decided to set up camp in the idyllic spot. As they turned up into the little valley where they had camped before, Mark gave a shout.

"Look!" he cried. "There's a horse loose over there!"

Everyone dismounted and approached the horse, which raised its head from the grass and nickered in greeting to the other horses.

"I think that's Norm's horse," said Posy. "Look, his saddle is over there."

Norm's horse had been untacked and hobbled, and it looked like Norm had made a start in setting up a campsite. However, all he had done was dump his gear near the creek and the children and Captain Gunn led their horses over to the pile of stuff.

"Golly," said Molly, rummaging through the bedroll and saddlebags. "I think I've found our things!"

And indeed she had. Captain Gunn closed his eyes and breathed a sigh of relief. His notebooks were there! He grabbed them, flipped through them, and declared that nothing was missing. Everyone else reclaimed their missing gear. The only thing still missing was Leticia's camera.

"He must have it with him," she said, "but where has he gone?"

Still holding their horses they did a quick look round, but found nothing. Norm seemed to have disappeared into thin air. They decided to unsaddle and hobble the horses and search up the hill where the horses couldn't go.

"Maybe he decided to take a look at the silver mine," said Harriet.

Fifteen minutes later the whole gang was once again climbing the hill, with poor Captain Gunn panting along in the rear. When he joined the rest of them in front of the abandoned mine, they could all see that something had happened to it. On their last visit the entrance had been closed off with a large piece of tin. That tin had been thrown to one side and the entrance gaped. With one accord, they all moved forward, but Captain Gunn stopped them from going too close. From where they stood, however, they could all see that the opening was now completely closed off by a pile of rocks.

"I think he must be inside," said Sophie. "Oh, poor Norm, he'll be so frightened if he's trapped."

No one could argue with that. If indeed Norm was trapped inside he must have realized that the hope of rescue was very slim.

"Be quiet, you lot," said Captain Gunn. "I'm going to go as close as I can and yell inside. Everyone listen for an answer."

Captain Gunn had a very loud voice and his shouts reverberated down the hill, where the horses all pricked up their ears and looked up.

After every yell, he put his finger to his lips and the whole gang listened, holding their breaths.

After the third yell, they all heard the very faint cry coming from the mine.

"Help! Help! I'm stuck!" came a faint voice.

Captain Gunn stood in thought for a few moments and then turned to the others.

"It's going to be pretty difficult digging him out with our bare hands, but we'll give it a try if there's no other option. I think we should scout around first and see if there's an easier entrance."

Sophie stayed by the main entrance, yelling every few minutes to Norm that they were all trying to get him out. The others scrambled farther up the hill over the entrance to the mine and spread out looking for any other way in.

Harriet noticed it first. She held up her hand and the others came over to where she was standing by a clump of bushes.

"I think I can hear Norm's voice coming up from those bushes, rather than the entrance."

"Careful," said Captain Gunn. "I don't want anyone falling down a hole and getting trapped with Norm."

On his hands and knees, he crawled closer to the bushes and started pulling them apart.

"Bingo," he cried. "There's a hole here, and I think it's an old airshaft. I'm going to yell down and see if Norm is anywhere near the bottom end of it."

With that, he cupped his hands and gave an enormous yell. There was an almost instant and surprisingly loud reply.

"I'm down here," said the voice, "and I can see a bit of light above me."

"Are you hurt?" called back Captain Gunn.

"I think I've broken my leg," came the reply. The voice sounded very young and seemed to be on the edge of tears. "Please, get me out!"

"Hang on there, we'll do our best, but we have to be careful—don't want to bring more of the roof down."

Captain Gunn crawled backwards away from the hole and called to Sophie to join them.

"There's no way we are going to get him out through this hole, so I'm afraid it's going to mean digging through the rock fall at the main entrance. I think we can probably lower him down some food and water, so I need one of you to go back down the hill and bring up a bag with a water bottle, food, and a piece of rope to lower it all down the hole. The rest of you, I want you to gather as many big sticks and branches as you can find. Digging through the rock is one thing, but we'll need to support the roof long enough to drag Norm out. If we can't manage it we may have to send a couple of us to the Douglas Lake Ranch for help, but I think we should give it a try first."

They had found their stolen property, and they had found Norm, but now the mission had changed from a hunt for a fugitive to a rescue operation. Their quarry had turned into a victim, and it was going to take the whole gang working as a team to get Norm out of his dangerous predicament. Molly felt vindicated at her distrust of Norm, who had not only been an accomplice in her being shot, but had now proved himself a thorough scoundrel and thief. However, she was not one to turn her back on someone in dire straits.

HALF AN HOUR later, they gathered by the airshaft again. They had a bag containing a water bottle and piece of bannock tied to a length of rope, which they had borrowed from Louis' packsaddle. Captain Gunn called down to Norm and then fed the bag down through the hole and lowered it by the rope. After a few moments they felt a tug at the end of the rope and it went slack, allowing Captain Gunn to pull it back up through the hole, minus the bag.

"Hang in there, Norm," he yelled down the hole. "We're going to start digging you out through the main entrance."

They retreated back down the hill to the blocked entrance, and Captain Gunn explained what they were going to do.

"I don't want anyone except me going near the entrance. The whole thing looks very unstable. I'm going to move a few rocks at a time and throw them backwards away from the entrance. When I ask for a prop I need you to throw me one from a safe distance. I'll shore it up as I go."

It was tedious and heavy work, and Captain Gunn had soon worked up a considerable sweat. He made progress, however, and at last they could once again see the entrance, although it was still blocked. An assortment of tree branches held up the roof, aided by old planks and bits and pieces from the rubbish lying around.

Suddenly, there was a rumble. Captain Gunn narrowly avoided getting buried as another portion of the entrance tumbled down. Fortunately, it had not completely undone the work so far, but Captain Gunn had had a narrow miss and came over to the children, brushing dust off his clothes and clutching a rock in each hand.

Suddenly he stopped and looked from one hand to the other, then sat down and studied the rocks closely.

"Come on, come on," urged Harriet. "We need to get Norm out. You can look at rocks later."

"Norm won't come to any more harm for five minutes," said Captain Gunn. "These rocks are very interesting, very interesting indeed."

He heaved himself to his feet and went back to the new rockfall, looking up at the roof and knocking off a couple more pieces with a piece of broken shovel. He came back to the others and laid his rocks out on the ground in a row.

To the children they didn't look any more or less like any of the other rocks that were lying around. Captain Gunn obviously saw something they didn't.

"I think those old miners might have given up five minutes too soon. If they'd taken one more swing at it, they'd have found this. Look, can you see what I'm seeing?"

The children gathered around and had a good look at the rocks. Upon closer inspection they could see that the dark grey rock contained a streak of slightly lighter grey material, which when Captain Gunn turned it towards the sun, gave off a slight sparkle.

"I've been in a good few mines in my time, mostly gold, but a few copper and one or two silver. Saw a huge one in Mexico a few years ago and the ore looked very much like this."

"What does it matter?" said Harriet. "Can we talk about silver once we've got Norm out?"

"Yes, of course," said Captain Gunn. "I think we're almost there, just a few more rocks."

Sure enough, another half hour's work and another dozen or so branches stuck in strategically, and Captain Gunn declared that they were ready to get Norm out.

"Someone go up to the air hole and tell him to crawl towards the entrance," said Captain Gunn.

Sophie scrambled back to the hole and called down to Norm.

"Can you crawl towards the entrance?" she yelled.

"Yes," came the reply.

Sophie joined the others a safe distance from the entrance. Captain Gunn was lying on top of the pile of rocks above which was a hole big enough for one person to squeeze through. After a few minutes he started backing up with his hands extended through the gap. Bit by bit, Norm emerged.

He was covered in dust and his face looked grey with tear streaks down his cheeks. His golden hair was filthy, and his clothes torn and covered in dirt. He crawled forward holding on to Captain Gunn's hands and finally collapsed at the feet of the children. His first words were oddly calm.

"Here's your camera," he said taking the strap back over his head and handing it up from the ground where he lay.

"What a cheek!" said Molly, with her hands on her hips. "That's not the only thing you stole, and you know it!"

"Shush, Molly," said Sophie. "We have our stuff back and now we need to figure out how badly Norm is hurt and get him back to the ranch."

"Please don't take me back there," said Norm, as tears poured down his face. "They'll call the cops and I'll end up back in jail."

"Let's start by getting you back down the hill where our nurse, Sophie, can take a look at your leg and do whatever first aid she can. Don't worry about the cops for now. We need to get you some medical attention first before we deal with what you've been up to," said Captain Gunn.

They were a long way from any outside help. It was up to Sophie and the others to figure out how to get him back to civilization without making his injuries any worse.

CHAPTER NINE

THE NURSE AND THE PROSPECTOR

Getting Norm down the hill to where the horses were grazing proved to be a challenge. He clearly could not put any weight on his injured foot, and the first attempts to use tree branches as crutches were unsuccessful. He'd go a couple of hopping steps, and the improvised crutches would slip and he would fall, yelping in pain. Eventually, Molly and Sophie, being about the same height, put their arms round his shoulders and supported him. For the really steep bits he sat down and slid on his backside down the hill, helped on all sides by the children.

Once they reached the bottom, and Sophie and Molly had him on one leg hopping towards Wee Tan's old firepit, things progressed better. Soon he was resting against a log with his legs stretched out in front of him. His left foot was bent at an odd angle, and Sophie surveyed it with trepidation.

"I think we should try to get his boot off," she said. "His ankle's obviously broken and if it swells up inside the boot it will make matters worse."

Norm went even paler and raised his tear-stained face to the group gathered around him.

"You should have just left me in the mine," he sobbed, looking no older than fifteen. "I've done a terrible thing robbing you, and I don't deserve your help."

"All right," said Captain Gunn, "don't worry about that for now. We'll try and get your leg more comfortable and then you can tell us why you stole from us. I mean, apart from Leticia's camera, nothing is worth much, except to us, of course."

Norm bit his lip and submitted stoically to Sophie's ministrations. Getting his boot off in one piece was impossible. Every time she tried to gently ease it off his foot, he yelped.

"We'll have to cut the boot off," she said. "Who has the sharpest knife?"

"That's my only pair of boots," said Norm. "If you cut one into pieces, I'll have to go barefoot."

"You won't be walking anywhere for a while," said Sophie, "and the best thing is to get your ankle in some kind of a splint so we can get you back on your horse and over to the ranch."

Norm held tight to Harriet and Leticia's hands and gritted his teeth, and Sophie, being as gentle as possible, cut through the leather of his very shabby boot and eventually eased it off his foot.

Inside his boot, he wore a filthy sock with big holes in the toes. Sophie had to breathe through her mouth as she cut through the sock and finally revealed the broken foot. It was very swollen and twisted at an odd angle.

"I don't know enough first aid to try to set it," she said. "I think the best I can do is stabilize it with a splint and bandage it as tightly as I dare. I don't want to risk cutting off the circulation."

Her recovered first-aid kit fortunately contained a couple of elastic bandages. With stout and flattish sticks on either side of Norm's ankle, Sophie was able to do a fairly good job of strapping his ankle so it couldn't move about.

"Does that feel any better?" asked Nurse Sophie, tucking in the ends of the bandages.

"Yes, thank you, Miss," said Norm. Some colour was coming back into his face, and he had stopped crying.

"We'd better make camp here, have something to eat, and get an early night," said Captain Gunn. "Tomorrow we'll hoist Norm on his horse and take it slowly back to the ranch. I think we can make it in one day. We made it here from the ranch with all those cattle on the first day of the drive, and I still think we'll be going faster than we were on our outward trip."

Molly and Mark soon had a cheering blaze going in Wee Tan's stone fireplace. Sophie managed to cook up a batch of bannock, which when served hot with a can of stew, was pretty tasty. After they had cleared up and were sitting around the fire, Captain Gunn turned to Norm.

"I think you'd better tell us your story," he said. "I haven't decided what we should do with you when we get you back to civilization, so let's hear what your excuses are for behaving in such a reprehensible fashion."

Norm wasn't too sure what reprehensible meant, but he got the gist of what Captain Gunn had said. After sitting quietly for a few minutes staring into the fire, he began his story.

"I was born in a little town on Vancouver Island called Cumberland," he began. "My dad worked down the coal mine, but he was killed in an explosion when I was four. My ma married again, and I have a little sister, Cath, who's twelve now. When I was eight and Cath was only two, my ma and stepdad were killed by a coal truck when they were crossing the street. We were put into separate orphanages, and I didn't see Cath until I ran away from my place when I was fourteen. Wasn't a nice place, I can tell you. We got starved and beat all the time. Anyhow, I ran away and managed to see Cath in her orphanage. She was eight by then and didn't seem to be doing too bad, but it just weren't fair that we couldn't be together. I figured I'd get myself a job and find a place to live and then we could get her out of that place she's in. I went down to Victoria and did odd jobs for a couple of years, but it was slim pickings.

"One day I went down to the docks looking for work. I was sleeping rough and feeling pretty desperate, when I met those guys off the *Black Pearl*. I knew they were bad 'uns, but I didn't have much choice. They said they'd feed and pay me a little to sign on as crew. Well, I did, and hated every minute of it. Weren't much better than the orphanage—I was always getting beat up.

"Well, you guys know what happened when we was shipwrecked and young Molly here ended up getting shot. I was arrested with the rest of the crew, but because I was only sixteen I got sent to a place for bad boys. It was a rotten place, too, but a bit better than being on the *Black Pearl* with those ruffians. Anyway, I got released last fall, and they found me a job at the Quilchena. No one there knows my past. Then you lot showed up. I recognized you soon enough and thought you'd tell Sam or Joe all about me, but you didn't. Freaked me out, though, that Molly kept after me. I thought she'd turn me in any minute.

"I'd thought I had a fresh start, but it just looked like I'd end up right back where I started—no job and no one ever wanting to hire me again."

At this Molly had the grace to blush. She realized that her attitude might have contributed to Norm's behaviour. It seemed he had lost hope.

"Then when I got to Fintry," Norm continued, "and the cattle were being loaded, I was sitting under a tree thinking I wasn't much nearer to getting Cath out of that home than I'd been before. I don't know what came over me—I just saw all your stuff lying there and grabbed what I could and took off. I'd not gone far when I figured I'd done a really dumb thing. How could I sell a bunch of notebooks and a camera without folks asking questions? I don't even know what those notebooks were about 'cause I can't read! Then when I got here, I just thought I'd go up and take a look at that mine. Maybe pick up some nuggets the old miners left behind. It was real stupid. You're all really nice and didn't shop me to Joe and Sam."

By now Norm was crying again and the others sat in silence thinking about his story. It was obvious to everyone that the difference between their privileged upbringing and that of Norm was as far apart as Scotland was from British Columbia. No one knew what they would have done if they had been in Norm's situation. And they could hardly believe that Norm couldn't read. They didn't know anyone over the age of six who wasn't already reading. Finally, Captain Gunn spoke up.

"All right, Norm, here's what we will do. We'll get you back to the Douglas Lake Ranch and I'll talk to Mr. Ward. We won't press charges for stealing our stuff." Here he gave Molly a stern look as he could see that she wasn't keen on letting Norm get away with it completely. "We'll try and figure out a plan for you once your leg is healed. For starters, you're not going to get far in life until you can read."

Norm could hardly believe that he wasn't heading back to jail, and his sobs began anew.

"Come along now, pull yourself together," said Captain Gunn. "Sophie here will take care of you, and I'm going back up that hill to take another look at the mine."

Captain Gunn must have really thought there was something worth looking at, because the effort involved in getting himself back up the steep side of the valley was considerable. He set off, with Molly, Mark, and Leticia accompanying him, while Sophie with Harriet and Posy stayed behind to look after Norm.

AN HOUR LATER Captain Gunn had brought out a pile of rocks from the mine and was picking up each piece in turn and turning it this way and that, trying to catch the evening sun and figure out if any of it was worth a hill of beans.

The others stood and watched him, and finally Captain Gunn spoke.

"I think what we have to do is stake a claim. I've heard that these claims expire, so it's worth a try to stake this one ourselves. Not sure what the protocol is here, but from what I've read about mining, I think we can do something that will stand up in court if it comes to a dispute. Once we get back to the Quilchena, our first stop will be the nearest mining office to find out the proper way to do this."

He got the children to gather some sticks that were of approximately the same height, as well as a pile of stones to prop them up as the ground was hard and they didn't have the means to drive the posts into the ground.

"I'm guessing here, but the number five hundred yards is ringing some bells," said Captain Gunn. "I think we need to pace out an approximate square that contains the mine and mark each corner with a post. Does anyone have a pencil with them?"

Leticia had a stub of pencil in her pocket, and Captain Gunn pulled his knife out of his pocket to shave a bare spot off each post.

"Does anyone have any ideas for a name for our mining company?" he asked, licking the tip of the pencil and preparing to write on the posts.

"We don't have a mining company," said Mark, stating the obvious.

"I know we don't," replied Captain Gunn, "but I think we'll have to form one to officially stake this claim."

"How about The Intrepid Mining Company?" said Leticia. "We've been pretty intrepid getting Norm out of the mine and discovering silver when everyone else thought it was all gone."

"The Intrepid Mining Company it is," said Captain Gunn as he painstakingly wrote their new company name and the date on each post. "Now, we'll try and locate the mine entrance in the middle of the claim, so let's put the first post about 250 yards downhill and west of the entrance."

The mine was not in the middle of a nice, flat, smooth piece of ground, but located in the hillside among rocks, steep slopes, and lots of undergrowth. But with a bit of difficulty they eventually pegged out an area about five hundred yards square, with the mine entrance approximately in the middle. Each post was secured to the ground by a pile of stones and the bushes had been pulled away so that they could be clearly seen.

"Now, to be on the safe side, I want Leticia to take a photograph of each post with all of us standing beside them," said Captain Gunn, who seemed to have acquired a new burst of energy and was busily organizing the staking and photographing of the claim.

Four photos were taken, with a fifth of the entrance to the mine for good measure.

"Well, I know it's a long shot, but you never know," said Captain Gunn. "Might be worth opening up and working this claim, and if it is you will all have a share in it."

Captain Gunn filled his pockets with some of the better looking rock samples, and the weary prospectors headed back down the hill to camp.

THE NEXT MORNING, when the campsite had been tidied, the
fire completely extinguished, and the horses saddled ready to
go, they had to figure out how to get the injured Norm back on
his horse. Eventually they led the horse alongside a big fallen
tree, and with one person holding the horse, two supporting
him, and Captain Gunn to give him a boost up into the saddle,
they got him up and settled on his horse. He could only use
one stirrup, so they were going to have to take it easy with no
trotting or galloping. The outward trek from the DLR to their
current campsite had taken the better part of a day. It wasn't
going to be much faster going back, even without the cattle.

Five hours later, after a brief stop for lunch, they were following the now clearly visible road downwards towards the
ranch. Leticia was the first one to notice a cloud of dust on the
horizon. It wasn't long before they could see that the dust was
trailing behind a pickup truck, which was quickly approaching
the group of weary riders. Posy and Leticia galloped ahead to
meet the truck as the others plodded along in their wake.

As the riders and the truck met, the two advance riders
could see Frank and Kenny Ward in the cab of the truck. It
looked like Sam had managed to contact the Wards by telephone and explain what had happened.

"Any luck?" called Kenny out of the passenger window.

"Yes," replied Leticia. "We've found Norm and we've got our
stuff back!"

"Wait until I get hold of that young scoundrel," said Frank
Ward grimly. "He's going to find himself in the lockup at the
Merritt jail before you can say 'Bob's your uncle.'"

"No, no," said Leticia, "wait until you've spoken to Uncle Bert before you clap on the handcuffs. We're not going to press charges, and in any case Norm is badly injured."

By this time the main part of the group had reached the truck. Everyone except Norm gathered round the Wards, who got out of the truck and leaned on the hood to talk to Captain Gunn.

"Right," said Frank eventually as he walked over to where Norm sat on his horse with his head hanging in shame. "It seems you chose a sympathetic bunch of victims to rob from. If it was up to me, I'd take you straight to Merritt, broken leg or no broken leg. Fortunately, you have a very eloquent champion in Mr. Cameron here. He insists we take you to the ranch and get a doctor—which you certainly do not deserve."

"Don't be too hard on him," said Sophie. "There's not really any excuse for robbing us, but Norm here has had a really bad time of it, and we have decided that it would be better to give him a helping hand than to punish him. He's already feeling bad enough about what he's done, so please, please be nice to him." She was almost in tears herself.

"All right," said Frank, "I see you've all decided to give Norm a break, so let's get him off that horse and into the back of the truck. I'm pretty sure Mrs. Ward will agree to take him in, and the first thing we'll do is phone for the doctor. There's a pretty good guy in Merritt who's got lots of experience patching up cowboys, so I'm sure he'll be able to fix Norm, no problem."

Norm was eased off his horse and laid out in the back of the wagon on top of his bedroll. The truck turned round and disappeared in its attendant dust cloud and the rest of them followed wearily in its wake.

A FEW HOURS later the children and Captain Gunn found themselves once again sitting on the porch at Frank and Kenny Ward's comfortable ranch house. Everyone had washed their extremely grimy hands and faces, but unfortunately they didn't have any clean clothes to change into and were a still a pretty grubby-looking crowd.

The doctor had been, and with Sophie and Kenny assisting him, had set Norm's ankle and put it into a plaster cast. Kenny and one of the resident cowboys had managed to clean Norm up and put him to bed in a pair of Frank's pyjamas. He was currently asleep after having been served a meal in bed. Never in his life had he been treated so well, and he was beginning to perk up and feel that there was hope for him after all.

As the rest of them enjoyed a drink on the porch before dinner, Captain Gunn was grilling Frank about mining and the staking of claims.

"I don't personally know much about it," said Frank, "but there is a mining office in Merritt and you can go there tomorrow after we get you back to the Quilchena. I also know of a few retired prospectors who live in the area; you should meet them and pick their brains. One of them, Clarence, can be found pretty much every day in the bar in the old hotel downtown."

"Right," said Captain Gunn, "it seems we have a plan with regards to the mine, but now I want to figure out what should happen to Norm. You've heard his story and I think you'll agree it's a pretty sorry one. I think he deserves a second chance, but I'll need your help."

"Okay," said Frank. "What's your thinking?"

"Well, I don't know how much you know about the Laird of Fintry," said Captain Gunn, "but I think he might be able to help us, or rather Norm."

"I know a bit about him," replied Frank. "He's a legend in the area, and of course we communicated about the delivery of those cattle. I know he's about to retire, so how do you think he could help Norm?"

"You may have heard about him handing everything over to those Fairbridge Farm people," continued Captain Gunn. "I know that Norm is a bit older than the kids they have brought out from England, but other than his age, he seems like a good fit for their program. I understand that the youngsters do lessons as well as learning about farming, and Norm needs to learn to read and write. I'll bet you that he will do very well there, and I think maybe we can persuade them to bring his sister to Fintry as well. They have several girls looked after by a house mother, and the girls learn farming skills as well as the boys."

"That's a great idea," said Kenny. "We'll keep him here until his leg heals and then hopefully we can transfer him over to Fintry. I'll give the Laird a call tomorrow. He's a real generous guy, and I think he will like the challenge of reforming Norm and taking his sister in."

THE NEXT MORNING the children were still asleep in their cabin when Kenny came knocking on the door.

"Posy," she said as the children raised sleepy heads from their pillows. The first night in a while on a mattress meant they had enjoyed a very good night's sleep. "Do you want a ride on Gandalf?"

Posy leapt from her bunk in excitement, and she and Kenny walked over to the barn where Gandalf was already tied to the hitching rail. Kenny had told Posy that he stood 16.2 hands high, and Posy was going to look like a pea on a drum when she was mounted on him. The woman and the child together brushed the splendid horse until his snowy white mane and tail rippled and his coat shone, and then Kenny saddled him, not with the side saddle she normally rode on, but with a beautiful English saddle.

"I thought you'd like to ride him English. He's very well trained, so I think you'll manage fine even without the Western saddle's horn to hang on to," laughed Kenny.

Posy wouldn't have dreamed of hanging onto a horn on any horse she rode—her riding skills were way beyond that. They led Gandalf out to a large corral and Posy mounted using the mounting block in the corner. With Kenny standing in the middle and coaching her, Posy spent an hour in horsey heaven. While she was riding, the others emerged from the cabin and

Posy called to Leticia to get her camera and take a picture. She posed for a couple of shots and then reluctantly dismounted and unsaddled the horse.

"Thank you so much, Mrs. Ward," she said. "That was an incredible experience, but Spotty is still my favourite."

EVERYONE TROOPED UPSTAIRS in the ranch house to say good-bye to Norm, who was looking and feeling much better after a good night's sleep and the competent ministrations of Mrs. Ward. He had been told about the Fairbridge plan and was waiting impatiently to hear that it was all arranged and that he and his sister, Cath, would be finally reunited.

"I promise to do you all proud," he said. "I'll work real hard, and once I can read and write, I'll send you a letter with all our news. You've given me a proper chance here and I won't let you down."

By now, everyone could see that Norm didn't have a mean bone in his body. His brief life of crime was misguided and mostly brought on by his tragic upbringing. Privately, Molly thought that was no excuse—not everyone who had an awful childhood ended up a criminal—but she was willing to take some responsibility for frightening Norm to the point that he had no other choice but to run away with their stuff. After all that, she had to admit that maybe sometimes leopards did change their spots. Or maybe Norm had been a good leopard all along.

BY MID-MORNING THE gang was once again mounted on their horses. After thanking the Wards for their hospitality, they headed down the road back towards the Quilchena Hotel. They all, for various reasons, were looking forward to being back there and the pace was brisk. Even Captain Gunn seemed to be at his best as he and Rocky trotted beside the lake. They crossed the bridge and continued along the road back to the comforts of the hotel.

CHAPTER TEN

TO MINE, OR NOT TO MINE

It was late afternoon when the weary troupe of horses and riders turned into the gravelled forecourt of the Quilchena Hotel. Rose and Arnold Schwimmer came hurrying out of the front door to greet them.

"I hear you've had quite an adventure," said Mr. Schwimmer, putting his fingers to his mouth and giving a piercing whistle.

A couple of cowboys the children did not recognise came running from behind the house.

"Take care of our guests' horses," said Arnold. "I think we can safely say they've had enough horse riding to last them at least a few days."

Even Posy was feeling tired, and after giving Spotty a hug and detaching her saddlebags, she handed over the reins to one of the cowboys. The others did the same and they all trooped into the hotel.

Sophie expressed what they all, to varying degrees, were feeling.

"I hope you don't mind, but we all really need a bath and clean clothes before we even sit down. I'd be afraid of leaving a dirty mark on the chair!"

Rose laughed. "You're back in the same rooms and I've had your luggage put ready for you. Off you go, and we'll join you in the bar for a drink when you're done. Kenny over at the Douglas Lake Ranch called me and told me what happened, but of course Arnold and I are dying to hear the whole story."

Captain Gunn headed directly to the bar, but Sophie grabbed his arm and gave him a stern look.

"You, too, Captain Gunn," she said in her sternest voice. "You're filthy! It's just not polite to be seen in a public place before you have cleaned up."

FORTY-FIVE MINUTES LATER, a totally transformed group of children came downstairs and went into the bar. Captain Gunn was already there. He had pulled his least disreputable outfit out of the bottom of his bag and added his jauntiest scarf around his neck. He probably would have been refused entry into a posh restaurant, but he looked a lot better than he had after a week spent on the trail.

Sophie regretted leaving the girls' frocks back at the Sylvia Hotel in Vancouver, but she had done her best with her sisters and made sure Molly, Mark, and Leticia did their best, too. They wore clean shorts and shirts, and everyone's hair had been washed. Mark's was damp and slicked down with a brush, and Sophie had insisted that all the girls plait their hair or tie it back. Molly had groaned but gave in.

They all found seats at the bar and ordered colas. Captain Gunn had an enormous tankard of beer and had already downed half of it. Cattle driving and prospecting were thirsty businesses, and they'd only drunk water and campfire coffee since leaving Fintry.

Rose and Arnold joined them, and everyone contributed various bits to the story of their adventures since leaving the Quilchena.

"I thought there was something shifty about that Norm," said Arnold. "We believed he had just grown up enough to leave the children's home—no one told us he'd been in juvenile detention."

"I think Norm is going to turn out all right," said Captain Gunn. "And you don't have to worry about him coming back here—at least until he graduates from the Fairbridge Farm programme and comes asking you for his job back!"

Talk turned to the mine and the possibility of it yielding anything valuable enough to justify the expense of working the claim. It was obvious that Captain Gunn was very keen on officially staking the claim and talking to anyone in the area who might be able to help.

"I suggest you go into Merritt tomorrow," said Arnold. "I'll give you a lift to the station in Nicola and you can take the train into town. First stop, I think, should be the mining office, and then go talk to Clarence in the hotel bar. Everyone around here knows him, and if anyone can help you, it's him."

"We'll need to get those photographs Leticia took developed to support out claim. Is there anywhere in Merritt that could develop a film?"

"Yes, there's a photographic studio on the main street. He's pretty good—takes all the photos of weddings and such around town, but it might take him a few days to get the film done."

"That's all right," said Captain Gunn, "we'll drop it off and can add them to our claim application later if we need to."

THE NEXT MORNING, the cowboys-turned-prospectors boarded the little train at Nicola.

"I'll come back and pick you up off the evening train," called Arnold as the train pulled away. "Good luck!"

Captain Gunn looked as if he'd like to get behind and push the train to make it go faster. He paced up and down in the space between the seats and kept peering out of the window to see how close they were.

Soon enough, the tiny train pulled into the station in Merritt, and Captain Gunn practically leapt onto the platform, gesturing to the others to follow him. He set a spanking pace but soon had to slow down and mop his brow.

"Don't worry, Uncle Bert," said Leticia kindly, "no one else will have had a chance yet to try and jump our claim. Still, we'd better keep a low profile until we've got it properly staked."

"You're right," said her uncle and managing director of the soon-to-be-formed Intrepid Mining Company. "Let's drop off your film and then find the mining office."

THE MINING OFFICE wasn't hard to find, being right on the main street, with a large sign saying "Mining Commission—District of Merritt." They mounted the steps and swung open the heavy door. Inside, the office appeared to be one large room with a wooden divider across the middle, similar to banks and post offices. They could see through the ornate metal railing that topped the wooden barrier, into the back half of the office. A long counter across the back wall was lined with cubbyholes filled with pieces of rock and on the counter large maps were either spread out and weighted down at the corners with spare rocks or rolled up in untidy piles. A man seated with his back to them tapped away at a typewriter. He turned when he heard the door close behind Captain Gunn and the children.

"How may I help you?" he said coming forward to the iron grille. He looked to be in his forties and was as thin as Captain Gunn was fat. He wore a shirt with no collar or tie and the sleeves rolled up and a pair of spectacles about as thick as the bottom of a cola bottle.

"I'd like to register a mining claim," said Captain Gunn.

"Well, you've come to the right place," said the man. "Do you know much about the mining business?"

"Some," replied Captain Gunn, "but I'm not sure about the rules here in Canada. I think the mine has been abandoned, but we seem to have accidentally uncovered a new vein of silver ore."

"Well, we'll need to make sure the claim actually has been abandoned before you can claim it for yourself. Why don't you come through and tell me all about it and we'll see if we can locate it on one of my maps."

There was a large table pushed against one of the sidewalls and the man, who introduced himself as Phillip Robertson, invited them to sit down while he sorted through his maps.

"A day's ride from the Douglas Lake Ranch, you say? Well, there were a few mines up that way and I'm pretty sure they've all been abandoned. The law says that you have to pay a fee each year to keep the claim active, and no one has paid any fees on mines in that area since I've been working here, and that's fifteen years."

Captain Gunn heaved a sigh of relief. It appeared that one hurdle had been passed—"'their'" mine seemed to have been abandoned and was therefore fair game for reclaiming.

Phillip found the map he was looking for and spread it out on the table.

"Right—here's the Quilchena and Nicola Lake and over here is the Douglas Lake Ranch," he said pointing to various spots on the map. "From the route you describe, I think your mine might be here—called the Blue Bell Silver Mine. You can see there's a notation on the map, and it means that the fees have not been paid. Hang on a minute, I'll look it up in the register."

Captain Gunn waited impatiently while Phillip went to a bookshelf under the counter filled with big red books with dates imprinted on their spines. He ran his finger along them and pulled out several.

"We'll start from the year before I came to work here and work backwards," he said flipping through the first of the books.

Ten minutes later Phillip stabbed his finger at an entry in one of the books and brought it over to the table.

"Last recorded as being worked and the appropriate fee paid in 1921—two years before I came to work here. You're free to

claim it as your own, providing you follow the proper procedure, of course."

Captain Gunn relaxed in his chair and pulled two pieces of
rock out of his pocket.

"What do you think of this?" he said. "Any chance we've hit
the mother lode?"

Phillip took the rocks and went over to his bench. He swung
a lamp over the rocks and took a magnifying glass out of his
pocket. He seemed to take forever inspecting the rocks, turning
them this way and that and scratching at them with a metal tool.

"Well, you'd have to take them to Kamloops and have them
assayed, but I think these rocks look promising. I don't know
how much you know about silver, but often it's found as a
bi-product of copper and other minerals such as gold, lead, or
zinc. This looks like it could be what they call native silver,
meaning it's found alone in the ore, not with any other minerals. Quite unusual. Now tell me exactly what you've done in the
way of staking the claim, and I'll tell you what else you have to
do to make it legal."

Everyone started talking at once, but Captain Gunn held up
his hand and the children subsided.

"We've staked out an area approximately five hundred yards
square and erected a post at each corner with the name of our
new mining company written on each post. We also took a
photo of each post and one of the mine entrance. What do you
think—is our claim legal?"

"You've got the basics right, and I think filing those photos
will add weight to your claim, but there are a couple of things

you need to do. One is attach a metal tag to each post—I'll give the correct ones to take away with you—and the second is to pay the official government claim fee. Then I think you should go and talk to Clarence Maw, who is usually to be found in the bar at the Coldwater Hotel in the middle of town. I'd suggest you be deliberately vague as to the exact location of the claim, since even if Clarence keeps mum, there are some pretty wide ears around, and who knows who might try to jump your claim before it is officially registered."

Everyone instinctively looked over their shoulders to see who was listening in, but they were the only ones in the room. However, Molly, who was the keenest of the children on the whole mining idea, looked sternly at the others.

"Cut your throats and hope to die," she said, making the age-old gesture of secrecy. "No one is to breathe a word about this to anyone who doesn't already know about it."

The children all solemnly repeated the oath. Meanwhile, Captain Gunn and Phillip had their heads together studying the map. Phillip reached into a drawer and pulled out four metal plates, about four inches square. Using the same sharp tool he had used to scratch at the rock samples, Phillip bent over the table and engraved the required information, including the date, and the names of their mining company and the Merritt office.

"You'll need to get back up there as soon as possible and nail these plates to the four posts you've pegged. It won't be legal until you've done that. In the meantime, to save time, I'll have you fill in this form and you will need to copy the portion of this map that contains your claim and draw in the boundaries of your claim."

"Harriet," said Captain Gunn, "you're the mapmaker and artist. Can you copy this part of the map?"

Harriet took a blank piece of paper and a pencil and carefully copied the bit of the large map containing their claim, including the old Blue Bell Silver Mine.

Meanwhile, Captain Gunn was filling out the forms, which he handed to Phillip along with the recording fee of five dollars.

"Best five-dollar investment I ever made," he laughed, "though I have a feeling that will be the only part of this endeavour that's cheap!"

"If you go and pay at the photographic studio, I'll pick up the photos once they are developed and add them to the claim. I'll keep the photos that aren't of the claim for you to pick up the next time you're in town," said their new friend. "You'd better go along the road and have that chat with Clarence, and then I suggest you hot foot it back to your claim, before anyone else does."

AFTER PAYING THE photographer, who promised to save Phillip a trip and deliver the photos over to the mining office the next day, the gang headed over to the Coldwater Hotel, which was a massive wood-framed building at the main crossroads in the middle of town. It had the most extraordinary brass cupola topping a circular tower that rose from the pavement where the streets crossed. The frontage was lined with posts at the edge of the street that created a shady area and held up a veranda on the second level of the hotel.

"Now, you lot," said Captain Gunn, "I want you to stay out here in the shade. I'll have some nice cold drinks sent out to you, but I don't want to draw attention to any meeting we may have with Clarence, and I'm sure there aren't too many crowds of kids piling into the saloon. In any case, since we're not staying here, I don't know what the rules are about children inside, so better to keep a low profile."

Captain Gunn dived into the cool of the saloon, which occupied most of the ground floor of the building. The ceiling was elaborately patterned painted tin, and the bar boasted a gleaming brass rail and massive mirrors in front of which were lined up what seemed like hundreds of bottles of liquor. Captain Gunn ordered himself a large beer and a small whisky and tipped the barman to take six bottles of cola out to the children. Scanning the bar, he casually asked the barman, once he got back inside, if he knew a Clarence Maw.

"Practically lives here," laughed the bartender. "He's over there." He pointed to the far corner by a window that gave a good view onto the street.

Captain Gunn walked over to the table where a grizzled old man sat sipping a small glass of beer and reading the paper. He looked every inch the miner (or what Captain Gunn imagined an old miner to look like) and had a huge white beard, denim shirt, jeans held up by suspenders every bit as colourful as Captain Gunn's, and heavy boots. His squashy felt hat sat on the table beside his drink, and it looked as if all he needed was a lantern and a hammer to get back to work in the nearest mine.

Captain Gunn introduced himself, got Clarence another drink, and sat down. They were soon deep in conversation.

AN HOUR LATER, the children outside were getting impatient. Eventually Molly went inside. He jumped up when he saw her approaching the table.

"Sorry, forgot all about you! Mr. Maw here has been a mine of information." He guffawed at this witty pun, clapped Clarence on the back, and went outside with his niece.

"All right, I'm not going to get into filling you lot in right now. We're going to have to run to catch the train, and you know me, I can't run and talk at the same time!"

They caught the train with moments to spare, were picked up by Arnold in the old farm truck, and by dusk were once again ensconced in the comfort of the Quilchena dining room enjoying another of Rose's excellent dinners.

Arnold and Rose joined them for coffee and Captain Gunn filled them in on his talk with Clarence.

"It seems he's pretty keen to get back into the mining business. He had a good guess as to where our mine was, but I think we can trust him to keep his mouth shut. We do, however, need to get up there first thing in the morning and attach our metal tags to the posts. Any chance of a lift up there in that old truck of yours, Arnold? I think Rocky has done his job of getting me to Fintry and back very well, and we should give him a break from having me bouncing up and down on his back! Not to mention that it's a long ride from here to the mine, and I think we can make it in a couple of hours by truck."

VERY EARLY the next morning, Captain Gunn, riding shotgun to Arnold, and Molly and Leticia riding in the back of the truck, set off for the mine. Their route followed that of the cattle drive; good road as far as the Douglas Lake Ranch, and then over the range on a track that would give everyone a bumpy ride. Molly and her sister had been the only two of the children who had wanted to go. Posy was going riding with her new cowboy friends, who had taken care of the horses when they had arrived back at the hotel. Their task was to check the fences for loose or broken areas in need of repair. Mark had discovered a vast equipment shed full of fascinating machines and was "helping" the resident mechanic, Cyril. Harriet would spend the day writing in her journal and working on some drawings she had started on the trail. Sophie was helping Rose and the maid Lily deal with the pile of laundry they had accumulated on the cattle drive.

BY LATE AFTERNOON, the children at the hotel were sitting in the shade of the willow trees. After the adventures of the past week, it felt good to relax and get their breaths back before Captain Gunn involved them in yet another adventure—as he surely would.

Posy glanced up at the sound of hooves and leapt to her feet as Sam and the Quilchena cowboys trotted into the hotel grounds. They were all there, except of course for Norm. Robert and George, the English mud pups; Thomas and Charlie, the trusty Native cowboys; and Gerry and Joey.

"So you got back safely, I see," said Sam. "Heard all about your adventures. We stopped briefly at the Douglas Lake Ranch on our way back from Westwold and had a chat with Mr. and Mrs. Ward."

Just as the cowboys were dismounting and preparing to lead their horses out back to the barn, the old farm pickup truck rattled in and Captain Gunn and Arnold got out. Molly and Leticia, wearing a layer of dust, climbed down out of the back of the truck. Sophie gave a mental sigh— she was going to have to do yet more laundry!

"How did you get on, Captain Gunn?" asked Harriet.

"Jolly good," replied the prospector. "Got those tags attached. Not much else to be done before I get Clarence up there to take a look at things. I'm ready for a bath and a drink. Thanks Arnold, hope you'll join me in the bar."

Although Uncle Bert was a very nice man with very deep pockets, Arnold was beginning to look forward to the peace and quiet that would hopefully descend on the hotel once his English guests had departed. Uncle Bert seemed to have stirred things up, what with participating in a cattle drive, being robbed, discovering a new lode of silver, and now wanting to be driven over very rough terrain to the mine. Arnold had already agreed to make the drive again the next day, or as soon as they could get Clarence out of the saloon in Merritt.

Sam returned from the barn and, when he had a nice cold beer in his hand and was sitting with the others in the bar, he made an announcement.

"We often get together with the other cowboys from neighbouring ranches and have a friendly contest. Calf roping, barrel racing, bucking horses—all great fun! So, how would you like to see a real cowboy rodeo before you leave?"

"That sounds incredible!" said Posy. "I don't suppose I could have a go at the barrel racing, could I?"

"Well, we have some pretty good racers in the area, but we could probably arrange one for you with the new cowboys that are still wet behind the ears," said Sam.

"What are your plans, Mr. Cameron?" asked Arnold.

"If I can get old Clarence up to the mine tomorrow or the next day, and he can give me an idea of what it's going to take to reactivate the mine, I think I'll head back down to Vancouver. I'll need to see a lawyer for one thing, to get this new company registered, and before too long I have to get this lot back across Canada to catch their ship home."

"I know when that ship leaves," said Molly, "and it's not for another two weeks. We were going to have three weeks in Vancouver after leaving here, but we've stayed an extra week. Still, what are we going to do in Vancouver while you are gadding around meeting lawyers?"

Captain Gunn tapped his nose and winked.

"You know me better than that," he laughed. "I love a surprise and you'll just have to wait and see what, if anything, I have up my sleeve!"

And with that they all had to be content. There was still the rodeo to look forward to and after that two full weeks doing who knew what before they had to be back on the *Empress of Britain*, heading back across the Atlantic.

CHAPTER ELEVEN
THE RODEO

The next morning the children awoke to a hotel and ranch humming with activity. Arnold and Rose sat down briefly with them over a cup of coffee to discuss the day's activities.

"I was able to get hold of Phillip from the Mines Office last night," said Arnold. "He said he'd go down to the hotel and find Clarence. He called me back this morning to tell me he'd just put Clarence on the train up to Nicola. So the mine visit is a go!"

Captain Gunn was thrilled and very appreciative of Arnold's help. They agreed to meet outside the front of the hotel in half an hour and drive down into Nicola to pick up Clarence. They'd be gone all day up at the mine.

"I'd sure appreciate some help in the kitchen," said Rose. "I'm going to be cooking up a storm for the rodeo tomorrow. We treat our neighbours like family round here, and we always get a good spread when we go visiting, so I'm planning to pull out all the stops for our guests."

Sophie, Leticia, and Harriet agreed to help Rose and Lily in the kitchen. Mark was delegated to find Sam and offer his services wherever they were needed. Posy had already arranged the day before to help a couple of the cowhands bring in some cattle off the range for the roping part of the rodeo. That left Molly, who volunteered to help one of the hands set up long tables in the shade at the side of the hotel, for the splendid feast that would be served after the rodeo.

Captain Gunn and Arnold roared off in the truck and everyone else got busy with the preparations.

The large corral where they had had their riding lessons was the main area for the rodeo, along with several adjoining, smaller corrals. Mark helped Cyril hook up a tractor to a set of wooden bleachers that were stored behind the barn, and they dragged them over and positioned them beside the big corral. They added benches, folding chairs, and bales of hay for extra seating. A string of gaily-coloured bunting was tacked up along the front of the barn, and a moveable cattle chute was drawn up next to the large corral, presumably to funnel cattle into the ring.

Posy rode in with the cowboys after rounding up a dozen or so cows with their calves. They would be used in the roping competition and would be branded at the same time—a competition based on the important ranch chore of identifying all the cattle belonging to the Quilchena with their particular brand. Posy was pretty sure she would not enjoy the calf branding as she knew it involved red hot irons applied to the calf's hide. However, she realized there was nothing she could do to change the way things were done on a cattle ranch; with her or without her, every calf on the ranch would eventually be branded.

She asked Sam what the smaller corrals were for.

"Well," he said, "we have a different way of breaking our horses. We don't do them the old-fashioned way by whipping and spurring them till they give in and stop bucking. Sure, we're going to have bucking horses in the rodeo, but they're bred special to buck and do the rodeo circuit. They're being trucked over from Kamloops. That's fun to watch, but don't feel bad for those horses—they're real good at their job and love pitching those cowpokes into the dust!"

"Yes," said Posy impatiently, "but what were you saying about your way of breaking horses?"

"Right, young Posy, you're going to really enjoy watching the breaking contest. We bring in three horses wild off the range, never even had a halter on them. And three of the best cowboys in the district get those horses to accept a bit and saddle and rider, all in the course of one day and all without using a whip or a spur. Very competitive it is. The crowd votes on the best broke horse and there's a prize. I'm one of the trainers, Joe from the DLR is another, and there's a guy from near Kamloops who's the third."

Posy was somewhat reconciled to the fate of the calves by the prospect of watching some gentle horse breaking. Certainly all the horses that had been along on the cattle drive were very well trained, and the cowboys seemed very fond of their horses and never used whips on them.

By late afternoon things were looking good. The main corral now had enough seating to accommodate the expected crowd, the tables and chairs for the feast were set up in the shade, a dozen pies were cooling in the larder, and half of a large metal barrel had been placed near the picnic area.

"What's that for?" asked Harriet, who was relaxing on the steps of the hotel after her day in the kitchen. The others trickled in from their various chores and joined her.

"That's for the barbeque," answered Rose, who was sitting on the porch with a cup of tea. "We'll be cooking a whole side of beef. The fire will be started tomorrow morning, and when we have a good bed of coals, we put the beef on that spit arrangement over the coals and it cooks all day. I baste it with my special sauce, and I can tell you that there's not much left by the end of dinner!"

Just then the old farm truck rolled in and Captain Gunn, Arnold, and Clarence piled out.

"How did it go?" called Leticia. "Did you pull out any huge silver nuggets?"

"You may well jest," said her uncle, "but Clarence here thinks we may have struck it rich. We're going inside to have a nice cold beer and talk about it some more. Come along all of you, I'll treat you all to a cola. Oh, and here's your packet of photos, Leticia. We left the ones of the mine with Phillip."

Everyone trooped into the bar.

"Well," Molly said to Clarence, after he had taken several huge gulps from his glass of beer, "what do you think? Are we all going to be rich, or is it just 'fool's silver'?"

Clarence was enjoying having an audience. In fact, even if nothing came of the mine, he was having a great couple of days being the expert and centre of attention.

"I think those old miners really did stop five minutes too soon," he began, "We had a good look at what your uncle here chipped away, and we managed to knock down a fair bit more rock. I used to mine down Princeton way twenty years ago, and I never saw rock that showed such good promise. It will take a fair bit of work to start mining again, but I think the investment might just be worth it."

"What's the next step?" asked Mark. "Do you just go up there and start chipping away?"

Captain Gunn laughed. "Not quite so simple," he said. "The first step is to get some samples to the assay office in Kamloops and see what they say. Then we'll have to do some pretty complicated sums to figure out if the expense of getting it out and processed is going to be worth it."

"I hope it's not going to spoil the rest of our holiday," said Molly, who had decided that if silver nuggets weren't just going to start rolling down the hill from the mine, she would rather be doing something else with the time she had left in Canada. "What's the plan? Are we going to hang around here while you play with rocks, or are we going to head back down to Vancouver?"

"Don't worry," he said, "I'm sending the samples to Kamloops with Arnold and Rose, who are going in for their fortnightly shopping trip at the end of the week. I need to get back down to Vancouver and see Mr. Goldstein to form that mining company, and he's the man for any sort of legal stuff."

"Jolly good," said Molly, eyeing her uncle. She knew better than to try and winkle any definite plans out of him, but she had a feeling that he had something better in mind than just sitting on the beach at English Bay.

"So," continued her long-suffering uncle, "we're heading back down to the coast the day after tomorrow. The rodeo tomorrow will be a great way to say goodbye to all our new friends."

THE NEXT MORNING dawned with a rosy pink sky and the promise of another fine and hot summer day. After a quick breakfast the children went outside to watch the final preparations for the rodeo. As noon approached, cars, wagons, and horses started arriving. Soon the area around the hotel was jam packed with an assortment of vehicles. A large wagon carrying the bucking horses had pulled up next to one of the corrals and the horses had been unloaded. They looked tame enough, but Sam told the children that they were the best buckers in the area, and it was a skilled cowboy indeed who could stay on board for the requisite eight seconds.

While the men in the crowd were staking out their seats next to the large corral, the women brought contributions to the feast and soon the kitchen was filled with a chattering crowd who had lots of local gossip to catch up on.

Soon, the crowd began gathering at the corral, and all available seats were filling up fast. Posy was over at the barn saddling up Spotty for the barrel racing, and the others, including Captain Gunn, were about to head over to the rodeo area and claim their seats.

"Oh, look," said Harriet, pointing over towards the road. "I wondered if Mr. and Mrs. Ward were coming, and I think that's their truck. Gosh, it looks like they've brought Norm with them!"

Sure enough, Frank Ward found a parking spot and jumped down from the truck, followed by Kenny, who leaned back in and helped Norm out, handing him a pair of crutches.

The three of them walked over to the children. Norm was almost unrecognizable. He was wearing new clothes and his curly blond hair had been neatly trimmed. The one boot he was wearing was red with designs stitched into the leather and a brass cap on the toe, and he was wearing a very nice-looking cowboy hat—a far cry from the battered filthy one he'd worn on the cattle drive. It looked like his stay with the Wards had done wonders for his appearance, but it was more than that. He no longer had the hangdog shifty expression he had worn before. He hopped up to them and doffed his hat.

"I was hoping I'd have a chance to thank you in person," he began. "It probably don't seem that way to you, but me stealing your stuff was the best thing that ever happened to me. I'm right glad you got me out of that mine, and I'm going to do everyone proud from here on. Mrs. Ward has starting to teach me to read, so I won't be a total dunce when I get back over to Fintry. I'm going the week after next when my cast comes off, and Mrs. Ward invited Cath to the ranch next week. We'll be able to get reacquainted before we start at Fairbridge.

"Now, there's one thing I have to do to really set things straight and that's go and tell Sam I'm real sorry for all the trouble I've caused."

With that he hopped off in the direction of the barns.

Sophie gazed after him with a bemused look on her face. Who could have imagined that the filthy, snivelling Norm, whom she had treated like one of her younger siblings, would have turned out to be so handsome?

Molly caught her look. "Looks like you might have found your first boyfriend," she quipped.

"Oh, shut up, Molly," said Sophie, blushing and turning away. Really, Molly could be so annoying. Just wait until *she* had a boyfriend—she'd give it back to her with interest.

THE RODEO WAS in full swing. Every available seat was taken, and more people lined the rails of the big corral. The children and Captain Gunn had found seats on the hay bales and were mostly enjoying the show, although compared to the restrained horse shows they had occasionally attended in England, some of the events seemed downright cruel. They had to keep reminding themselves that these rodeos were a friendly contest between cowboys who used these very skills all the time in their working lives.

The calf roping competition had wrapped up. One of the cowboys from the Douglas Lake Ranch won the contest with a roping time of eleven seconds. The roped calves had been branded by a team of cowboys, and the whole procedure—the calf bolting out of the chute, being lassoed and tied by the competing cowboy, being branded, freed, and let out of the other end of the corral to join its mooing mother—was less than thirty seconds. It might have been rough and ready, but at least it was over quickly.

The next event was the cutting competition, where the cowboys formed teams from their home ranches. The idea was to "cut" a calf out of a group of calves and get it into a cattle chute. Each calf had a number whitewashed onto its back, and as the cowboys lined up at one end of the arena, a random number was called out through the megaphone. The cowboys displayed incredible horsemanship and cattle handling ability, as they efficiently separated their calf out of the herd and drove it towards the chute. Two of the cowboys then jumped off their horses and manhandled the calf to the finish line—into the chute with the gate closed. The crowd cheered and yelled as each team took their turn. It was tight, but eventually the Quilchena cowboys won by twelve seconds.

There was also a wagon race that started and finished in the corral, but which took the four teams along a wide trail about half a mile from the ranch, around a barrel, and back to the corral. Wee Tan, crouched on the seat with his pigtail flying behind him, won handily to cheers from the Quilchena contingent.

The bucking contest was a huge hit with everyone. The competitors flew around the ring, holding on with one hand to the strap roped around the horse's middle, while the buckers twisted, crow hopped, and bucked their hearts out. As soon as the horses had unseated their riders, they stopped and stood still in the middle of the corral, as if taking a bow. Their former minder on the cattle drive, Gerry, won. His prize was the most splendid pair of sheepskin chaps that made him look like some mythical creature—human on the top half and hairy sheep on the bottom half!

Finally it was time for the barrel racing. There were several heats of experienced cowboys pitted against each other. The idea was for the horses to gallop into the ring, race a cloverleaf pattern around a series of three barrels, and then race out of the ring at full gallop. A timer stood near the gate with a stopwatch. The competition was fierce, but eventually Thomas from the Douglas Lake Ranch won. Posy had begged to be allowed to try this sport, and Sam called round to a few of the local ranchers to bring some of their kids and ponies. There were four children for Posy to ride against, and she had drawn last place. She rode Spotty at a gentle trot near the barn to warm him up, without wearing him out.

The first boy, followed by his sister, rode the barrels in twenty-eight and twenty-nine seconds, respectively; the third rider, another girl, in twenty-six seconds; and the last boy in twenty-four seconds. That was the time for Posy to beat.

There was a hush as Posy prepared to start her run. She jammed her hat firmly down on her head, took up the reins, leaned down and whispered in Spotty's ear, then sprang forward at a full gallop. The timekeeper clicked his stopwatch as she sped into the corral and then the crowd started to cheer, the English contingent yelling and whooping and hollering with the rest. Posy appeared glued to Spotty's back, and neck reining in true Western fashion, as well as using her body and legs to guide her pony through the turns, sped around the barrels, coming within a hair's breadth of each. As she made the final turn and began her run for the gate, the crowd was on its feet. It looked as if Spotty's hooves weren't touching the ground as Posy flew past the timekeeper and pulled to a halt a short distance away.

The man with the stopwatch ran over to Arnold, who was on a stand with a megaphone announcing the names of competitors and winners. After a brief consultation, Arnold held up his hand for silence.

"The winner of the children's barrel racing competition is . . . Posy Phillips, with a time of twenty-three seconds!"

Posy came back into the ring and did a victory lap. She was the happiest she had ever been, and even though she knew that finally she would be parting from Spotty, the bonus of the last week was enough to make the parting bearable.

The horse-breaking contest had been going on all day at some distance from the main corral. Sam, Joe, and a neighbouring rancher had each been assigned a wild horse that had been brought in off the range. These horses had never even been haltered, much less ridden. Since early morning, the three men in their separate corrals had been working with their horses. Spectators taking a break from the main events in the big corral would wander over and take a look to see how the competitors were getting on.

It was really incredible to watch the three experienced horsemen working with their horses. They worked with their voices, a long rope attached to the horse's halter, and a stick with a torn piece of sacking on the end. The stick was not used to whip the horses, rather to encourage them to move out freely around the corral. Once they had got the horses listening and obeying directions to move, halt, and turn, the trainers started to accustom the horses to a saddle blanket, patting the horses backs with the blanket, sliding it on and off until the horses did not take any notice. Next came the saddle, which was a little harder, but the patient trainers took it slowly and soon the horses accepted the saddle and allowed the girth to be cinched.

By the middle of the afternoon, the three horses were saddled and moving around their individual corrals. The trainers slapped the stirrups against the horse's flanks until they were taking it all for granted, looking to the trainers to tell them what to do next. The big moment for each trainer came when they attempted to mount their horses. First they just had one foot in the stirrup, then they leaned their weight across the saddle, and finally the moment came when they put their other leg over the horse's back and sat in the saddle. The audience clapped softly, not wanting to startle the horses, but it really was an accomplishment worthy of applause. A totally wild horse had been tamed and ridden within a few short hours.

The training competition was decided after all three horsemen had brought their horses into the arena and put them through their paces in front of the judges and the crowd of spectators. All the trainers had done an incredible job, but Joe Coutlee from the DLR won by a small margin. He was able to walk, trot, canter, and back up his horse without it spooking at the now openly cheering crowd.

It had been the most splendid day, and it wasn't over yet. Everyone gathered at trestle tables set out under the trees and enjoyed a feast which Mark later described as "the best meal ever!" He grinned an apology at Sophie, and added that her meals were almost as good. After everyone had eaten their full, the party moved over to the firepit. As dusk fell and the light faded, the singing cowboys brought out guitars and banjos and everyone joined in on song after cowboy song. It really was the perfect end to their cowboy adventures.

THE NEXT MORNING began with a flurry of activity as bags were packed and goodbyes said.

"I'm going to have a last check in everyone's room," said Sophie as the gang stood in the lobby with their bags. "I know you're supposed to be grown up, Captain Gunn, but we know how forgetful you are, and what a bad packer."

"I have to say a last goodbye to Spotty," said Posy, who was already almost in tears at finally having to part from her beloved pony. "My prize money from the barrel racing is going to buy him a new halter. I've picked out a lovely one with a studded nose band, and the lady in the shop says she can have a metal plaque engraved with his name."

"All right, but hurry up. Mr. Schwimmer is going to be here with the wagon any minute," said Sophie.

Posy rushed around the side of the hotel to the corral where Spotty was enjoying a relaxing morning with a pile of hay. She flung her arms around his neck and buried her face in his mane.

"Don't worry, young Posy," said Gerry as he came out of the barn. "We'll take good care of him for you."

Posy gave Spotty a last kiss on his velvety nose and hurried back to the others. Arnold was just pulling up in the farm wagon and everyone piled their luggage and themselves into the back. Posy rode on the driver's seat with Arnold.

Rose and some of the cowboys who had got wind of the departure lined the steps in front of the hotel, and the last thing the children saw as the wagon pulled away were their friends, waving and yelling goodbye. It had been an epic adventure, and who knew what plans Captain Gunn had cooked up for the remaining two weeks they had in Canada.

TWO DAYS LATER they found out. They had taken the train back to Vancouver and were comfortably ensconced in the Sylvia Hotel once again. The day before they had sorted out all their luggage, including the stuff they had left behind when they left for the Interior. They lazed and swam at the beach, walked in the park, and enjoyed a marvellous dinner at Mr. Chen's excellent restaurant. As they sat down to breakfast on the second day of their return to the coast, Captain Gunn made his announcement.

"I didn't want to tell you the news until I was sure," he said as he enjoyed his second cup of coffee, "but I just got a telephone call from our old friend, the owner and skipper of South Islander, and he's agreed to let us charter her again. We're going to have ten days of sailing before you have to leave for England."

The children were too well bred to yell and cheer in a public place, but they were all thrilled by this news and chattered happily about this unexpected bonus holiday within a holiday.

"Where shall we go, Uncle Bert?" asked Leticia. "I don't suppose we have time to go back to Desolation Sound."

"Quite right, Leticia, with only ten days we'd just about get up there before we'd have to turn around and head back for you to catch one of Jim Richardson's cargo planes back to Montreal. No, I thought we'd have a nice relaxing cruise around the Southern Gulf Islands, maybe duck down into the American San Juan Islands, or perhaps into Victoria. Now, I have to go and meet Mr. Goldstein about setting up our mining company. While I'm gone I'd like you to get your stuff organized for ten days at sea. You won't need your cowboy hats or boots! Sophie, I'm putting you in charge, but you are not to do the work, understand? You sit yourself down and order the rest of this ungrateful lot around! We all know that our adventures would be a great deal less comfortable without you, so the rest of you take note and give the poor girl a rest!"

TWENTY-FOUR HOURS LATER *South Islander* pulled away from her old slip in Coal Harbour, and the crew motored out towards English Bay.

"Holy smokes!" exclaimed Molly as the gap between Stanley Park and West Vancouver hove into view. "How on earth did they do that?!"

They all gazed in awe at the bridge that now spanned the First Narrows. It really was an incredible feat of engineering, soaring in a huge sweep from north to south, and appearing to hang on what looked like the slimmest of cables. They could hardly believe that it could support the lines of traffic that would soon roar back and forth across it (Captain Gunn had told them it would be open to traffic in a couple of months). As *South Islander* passed under it, the crew looked upwards at the tiny figures putting the finishing touches to what was surely one of the most impressive bridges anywhere in the world. Leticia took a photograph to add to her collection and then the crew left the bridge and the city astern and looked ahead across the sparkling waters of the bay. Cattle driving and mining exploration may be behind them, but they still had ten days of holiday to look forward to, and what better way to spend them than cruising the beautiful waters of British Columbia?

EPILOGUE

Captain Gunn did not make it home to An Cuileann that Christmas, but everyone else did, including Ian, on leave from his first navy posting. The Phillips family had once again been invited to make the long trip north from their home in Devon for the holiday.

Mrs. MacTavish had recently heard from her brother and filled them in on what had been happening in Vancouver since the children had made the six-thousand-mile trip back home to England four months earlier.

"It seems that the Intrepid Mining Company is up and running," she said as they gathered in front of the fire, cozy behind the new double-glazed windows installed with the help of Brother XII's treasure. "Bert has made several trips back up to Merritt and the mine is now a going concern. They've improved the road to the mine and built a tramway to get the ore down the hill. There's a crushing plant there, too, and then the silver is sent by truck and train to a town called Trail for smelting. It seems that the local economy has taken quite a boost from reopening the mine and my dear brother is somewhat of a celebrity in the area!"

"Well, don't keep us in suspense," said Molly to her mother. "How much money is the mine going to make, and more to the point, how much are we each going to get? I'd love to take two flying lessons a week instead of one!"

Molly's mother laughed, but she knew that none of her children were mercenary and that money wasn't going to spoil them.

"He isn't sure how rich it's going to make you all," she said, "but he wanted me to tell you how he's set up the company. He's given himself a 65 percent share in the company, which is only fair since he's doing all the work. The six of you that were there when the silver was found are going to get a 5 percent share each. Sorry, Ian. I'm afraid you're not in on this one!"

Harriet was the first one to notice the discrepancy.

"Six shares at 5 percent is only 30 percent," she said. "What about the remaining 5 percent?"

"Bert thought you would all agree that Norm should get a share, since without him getting stuck in the mine you'd never have discovered the silver," said Mrs. MacTavish. "What do you think?"

The children sat silently for a few minutes pondering the ethics of Norm benefitting, even indirectly, from stealing their possessions. Eventually Sophie spoke up.

"I think that it's a jolly good idea. Any extra money that Norm makes from the mine will help him set up home with his sister. We're all lucky and don't really need the money, but even a little will mean a lot to Norm."

She actually knew more about Norm and his sister than she was letting on. Soon after their return to England, she had received a letter from Kenny Ward at the Douglas Lake Ranch and enclosed in the envelope was a note from Norm—the first letter he had ever written. As his writing skills had improved, the correspondence between him and Sophie had continued with longer letters describing his new life. Sophie, knowing she would be teased if anyone knew about this, kept his letters to herself. She knew it was unlikely to happen, but she would really like to see Norm again one day.

With the thought of what may be possible for all those involved if the mine was a success, they all raised their glasses in a toast to the absent Captain Gunn and the Intrepid Mining Company. One adventure may have ended but they knew that there would be many more to come.

ACKNOWLEDGEMENTS

Thank you to Ken Mather for writing such informative books about the history of cattle ranching in BC and for taking the time to answer my questions and give me a personal guided tour of the O'Keefe Ranch.

Robin at the Princeton Museum gave me access to the basement of the museum, where I was able to find samples of silver ore and documents relating to the history of mining in the area.

Barbara Bell at the Vernon Archives was extremely helpful and found me articles and cuttings that make the Laird of Fintry a historically accurate character. She also struck pay dirt by digging out a government-issued booklet, which told me everything I needed to know about staking a claim.

Helen Kennedy at the Hope Museum researched information about silver mining and processing.

Ray Martin, who has been flying the skies of British Columbia for over fifty years, told me what type of plane to send Molly flying in, and much about the history of Canadian aviation.

Julie Oakes and her daughter, Greta, reacquainted me with their beautiful property, High Farm. It really is a little piece of Paradise.

Joel Ashburner gave me information on the geology of mining.

Finally, thanks to the staff at Heritage House, in particular Lara Kordic, Leslie Kenny, and Lenore Hietkamp.

On the following pages,
read an exclusive preview of
***Up in Arms*,**
the exciting sequel to
The Silver Lining!

Coming soon from
Heritage House Publishing

CHAPTER ONE
EVACUATION

March 1940

"I'm not going," said Molly, stamping her foot.

Her mother sighed, took a deep breath, and tried again.

"I know you want to help with the war effort, but you're still too young. You have another term at school and you will be much more use if you finish your education."

"I'm seventeen, and I can fly," said Molly, sticking her lower lip out mulishly and looking about twelve.

"I hardly think they'll let you join the RAF and fly a bomber," chuckled her mother, "but in any case, there are other reasons for this."

"This" had been a letter from Fiona MacTavish's brother, Bert Cameron, back once again in Vancouver. At the outbreak of war the previous September he had been recruited by an unnamed and secretive Government department to liaise with a Canadian committee based in Victoria, BC. He was not at liberty to divulge the nature of his work, but his family did know that he was enjoying himself immensely, working with similarly eccentric men and combining their impressive brain-power on secret projects.

"Your Uncle Bert thinks that things are going to get a great deal worse for us here in Britain. He fears a massive air offensive by the Germans and we really are not too far from the dockyards in Glasgow, which will be a prime target."

"Mother, that's just rubbish," exclaimed Molly. "We're miles from Glasgow and unless those Germans are stupider than we think, even they couldn't be so far off target as to be dropping bombs on us here in Plockton."

The MacTavish home was on the west coast of Scotland, beside a large sea loch dotted with islands. It was a great place to sail and explore, and a wonderful place to grow up. It was remote enough, but Mrs. MacTavish knew from her brother's letter that bombers often went astray, missed their targets, or simply dumped bombs on their way back to their home bases. Plockton was only about a hundred miles as the crow flies from the major city of Glasgow. It seemed perfectly safe, but people were beginning to get the sense that nowhere in Europe was safe.

Leticia had been quiet during this exchange, but now she spoke up.

"I think we should listen to what Mother has to say," she said. "Uncle Bert knows a lot more than he lets on, and if he thinks it's a good idea, we should at least think about it. I'm not too keen on having bombs dropped on us, I can tell you!"

"Oh, all right," said Molly ungraciously, "If Uncle Bert wants us to turn tail and hot-foot it back to Canada, I'll consider it!"

Her mother stopped herself from pointing out that Molly really didn't have much choice. She was still technically a child and had to do what her mother thought was best for her and her sister and brother. Knowing her daughter as well as she did, however, she decided to allow her the notion that she had some part in making decisions for the MacTavish family. Growing up with only a mother and an eccentric uncle (their father had died many years before), the MacTavish children had been brought up to make their own decisions, guided but not dictated to by the adults in their lives.

"Right, this is what he wants us to do," said Mrs. MacTavish. "Apparently there are plans afoot by our government to evacuate children across the Atlantic to Canada and America. Those plans are not finalised yet, and Bert doesn't want us to wait until they are. He's arranged a passage aboard your old friend *The Empress of Britain*, for us four as well as the Phillips children."

Molly jumped up in excitement.

"Well, that changes things," she said. "It'll be like old times—all of us on another adventure!"

"Yes, it certainly will be an adventure," said her mother, deciding not to mention the risk of crossing the Atlantic in wartime. Molly was the bravest child she knew, but Leticia was younger and more sensitive. Their brother, Mark, was now almost sixteen and would no doubt see the journey as more thrilling than any of the boys' adventure stories he was addicted to.

"Mrs. Phillips will be staying in England," continued Fiona. "You know that Commander Phillips now has a very important desk job with the Navy, and Ian is at sea on a destroyer patrolling the English Channel. She wants to be close for when he gets shore leave, but she is happy for Sophie, Harriet, and Posy to join us. The *Empress* has been turned into a hospital ship and will be crossing to Canada to pick up a contingent of Canadian doctors and nurses to staff the ship, but on the way over they are taking families and some unaccompanied children to live in Canada for the duration of the war."

Molly wasn't giving in quite so easily. She sensed she might have some bargaining power here.

"Well," she said, "I might consider it if I could have flying lessons when I get there."

Molly had been taking flying lessons for three years, when she had turned fourteen and was able to get a student permit. She had been inspired by their first adventure in Canada when the legendary BC coast pilot Jim Spilsbury had flown her to hospital after the villains on the *Black Pearl* had shot her. This had happened during their Brother XII adventure, when they had recovered a king's ransom in gold coins. She was close to getting her pilot's licence, but all recreational flying had been stopped when war had broken out the previous September.

Her mother appeared to consider this request, but in fact her brother, knowing his niece as well as he did, had written in his letter that he thought it would be easy for Molly to resume her flying lessons in Canada.

"Mmmm…well, we'll think about it, but if you don't put up any more fuss and help me and your sister get things organized,

I think your uncle may be able to arrange lessons for you when we get there."

Molly gave in. Maybe sitting out the war in British Columbia, with its opportunities for adventure and the chance to get back in the air, wasn't such a bad idea.

Discover a world of action and adventure on the high seas with *Brother XII's Treasure!*

Available now from Heritage House Publishing

heritagehouse.ca

ABOUT THE AUTHOR

FTER A CHILDHOOD spent in England, where she attended boarding school and teacher training college, AMANDA SPOTTISWOODE immigrated to Canada in the 1970s and settled on Salt Spring Island in 1995. In 1997 she co-founded Graffiti Theatre Company, which she ran for fifteen years before retiring in 2012.

Adam Gilmer, Lightwell Photography

As a child, Amanda was taught to sail by the Royal Navy on the River Thames. After moving to Salt Spring, she finally realized her childhood dream of sailing and exploring a rugged coastline by boat. Amanda and her husband, Tom Navratil, have spent every summer since 1998 cruising on their thirty-four-foot wooden sloop, *South Islander*, exploring the waters between the Southern Gulf Islands and the north end of Vancouver Island. These travels were the inspiration for her first children's book, *Brother XII's Treasure*.

Amanda has two children—a daughter who lives in Geneva with her husband, and a son who is a professional photographer and lives with his wife in Victoria—and two grandchildren.

ARTIST, SET DESIGNER, and travel-ler MOLLY MARCH has painted and designed theatre sets for operas, ballets, and plays all over the world—from Hawaii to London and from British Columbia to Chile. She has been creating shows with BC theatre companies Runaway Moon Theatre, Caravan Farm Theatre, and Leaky Heaven Circus for the past thirty years. Molly illustrated Amanda Spottiswoode's first children's book, *Brother XII's Treasure*. She lives in Coldstream, BC.